Also by Scarlett St. Clair

When Stars Come Out

HADES X PERSEPHONE
A Touch of Darkness
A Game of Fate
A Touch of Ruin
A Game of Retribution
A Touch of Malice
A Game of Gods
A Touch of Chaos

ADRIAN X ISOLDE
King of Battle and Blood
Queen of Myth and Monsters

FAIRY TALE RETELLINGS
Mountains Made of Glass
Apples Dipped in Gold

APPLES
DIPPED IN
GOLD

A
FAIRYTALE
RETELLING

SCARLETT ST. CLAIR

Bloom books

To Christa's she shed

Copyright © 2024 by Scarlett St. Clair
Internal design © 2024 by Sourcebooks
Cover design by Regina Wamba
Cover images © Pixelsquid/Shutterstock, Prostock-studio/Shutterstock,
Pelagija/Shutterstock, Marinesea/Shutterstock, natrot/Adobe Stock,
Pierell/Adobe Stock, Vera NewSib/Adobe Stock, roman3d/Adobe
Stock, Nabodin/Adobe Stock, Alexey Pavluts/Adobe Stock
Internal art by Lauren Boyle
Map illustration by Meri/Ceban Art

Published by Bloom Books, an imprint of Sourcebooks
P.O. Box 4410, Naperville, Illinois 60567-4410
(630) 961-3900
sourcebooks.com

Cataloging-in-Publication data is on file with the Library of Congress

Printed and bound in Canada.
MBP 10 9 8 7 6 5 4 3 2 1

Content Warnings

This book contains themes of physical abuse of humans and animals, mental abuse, suicide, and violence.

If you are a victim of domestic violence, please call the National Domestic Violence Hotline at 1-800-799-SAFE (7233) or visit www.thehotline.org

If you or someone you know is contemplating suicide, please call the National Suicide Prevention Lifeline at 1-800-273-TALK (8255) or go online to suicidepreventionlifeline.org

Are you a survivor? Need assistance or support?

National Sexual Assault Hotline 1-800-656-HOPE (4673) hotline.rainn.org

Have you witnessed or experienced child abuse?

The Childhelp National Child Abuse Hotline Crisis can help.

Call 1-800-422-4453 or go to childhelphotline.org

The Kingdom
of Larkspur

The Kingdom
of Havelock

The Kingdom
of Hellebor

The Glass

The King
of Nightsh

The
of

The Em

Gnat

Rook

Cinder

Iron Haven

Sable

Fawn

Oak

Holle

Linden

The Seven Brothers
& Their Seven
Kingdoms:

The Seventh, Casamir: The Kingdom of Thorn
The Third, Lore: The Kingdom of Nightshade
The First, Silas: The Kingdom of Havelock
The Sixth, Eero: The Kingdom of Foxglove
The Fourth, Talon: The Kingdom of Hellebore
The Second, Cardic: The Kingdom of Larkspur
The Fifth, Sephtis: The Kingdom of Willowin

CHAPTER ONE
Three Wicked Brothers

SAMARA

I stood at the center of Daft Moor staring into the endless night, made darker by the thick tree line of the Enchanted Forest. It grew so tall, it blocked out the moon and stars. The ground beneath my feet was soggy and cold as ice, the frosty air smelled rich and sweet, and blood stained my hands. It felt thick and seeped between my fingers to the ground, splashing my bare toes like raindrops. I refused to look at the pool of crimson gathering at my feet. I did not want to face what I had done. Knowing was enough.

The blood was not my own.

It belonged to a fae I had once almost loved but had betrayed on this very moor.

My heart ruptured with guilt, carving a painful path from my chest to my throat.

The ache woke me, and when I opened my eyes to the dark, a fresh wave of grief roared to life. I was used to the feeling. I had dreamed the same dream for the last seven years, coaxed into slumber by a haunting voice whispering my name.

Samara, it sang. *Samara, my love, come to me. Flee with me. I can set you free.*

But those words were nothing more than a broken promise, and each morning when I woke to the same heavy darkness, I was left alone to face my punishment for the wrong I had committed before the Enchanted Forest.

I sat up slowly, my lower back aching as I threw my legs over the side of my bed, though calling the pallet I had built up in the corner of the kitchen "a bed" was quite an exaggeration. Still, it was better than sleeping on the floor where the rats could reach me.

I shivered at the thought and looked down at my hands, which were also sore. I spent yesterday bent at the waist for hours, cutting into packed layers of peat. I had been working little by little each day, hoping to harvest enough for the coming winter, though it promised to be long and harsh. I might have harvested more had my three burly brothers helped, but it was not a task that fell to them. No task fell to them.

That thought brought a wave of guilt. I knew I was being unfair. My brothers—Jackal, Michal, and Hans—might not help with the house or the animals or harvest peat, but they did hunt, and they were the greatest hunters in all of Gnat. Only they managed to enter the Enchanted Forest and return with spoils—spoils that kept the entire village fed.

They were heroes, and I was nothing more than what *they* made me, because I could be nothing else with the blood of the fae on my hands.

"Your fingers look as if they have been dipped in blood," my brothers had said upon first seeing my hand. "You will be marked for shame by the villagers and death by the fae, but if you will listen to us always, we will keep you safe."

I believed them at first and had been scared enough to listen, but as the days passed, one after the other harder than the last, death did not seem so dreadful.

In fact, I had begun to think favorably of it. There was something beautiful about ceasing to exist—something that sounded a lot like...rest.

Shame burned my cheeks. I should not think of resting while so many suffered around me, and now, as winter drew near, it was imperative everyone pulled their weight, especially me, who had the responsibility of ensuring the three greatest hunters of Gnat were well rested and well fed.

It was that obligation that drew me from bed.

There was a chill in the air that made my flesh prickle. Still, I crossed to a table in the corner and poured icy water into a bowl and splashed my face. The cold shock roused me, and I dressed in warm layers before kneeling before the fireplace where embers glowed beneath white ash. I raked everything into a pile and reached for the bucket I kept near the fire that was supposed to be full of kindling, except it was empty.

Strange.

I knew I had gathered branches and bits of bark before dusk to keep from having to do it this morning.

Anger twisted in my gut. One of my brothers must have taken it.

"Ladies do not get angry," I heard my mother say. *"It is unbecoming."*

My teeth ached as I fought to quell what felt like violence in my veins and rationalized their behavior.

Perhaps one of them had grown too cold in the night, used all their kindling—which I had also refilled—and came for more. After all, if they did not sleep, they could not hunt, and if they did not hunt, we would not eat, and if we did not eat, we would all die.

I sighed and tossed the rake aside. It clattered to the ground as I swiped the bucket from the floor and ventured into the semidarkness. The cold felt like a fist pushing on my chest. It hurt to breathe, but it was a familiar feeling.

As I stepped out onto the frozen ground, I thought I could smell snow coming. There was a sharpness to the cold—like knives poised against my skin.

I made my way across the yard to the wood I kept piled near the barn. As I gathered juniper, pine, and a few large pieces of oak, a slim black cat hopped onto the heap, stretching and purring, eager for attention.

"Good morning, Mouse," I said, scratching behind her ear. "Have you roused Rooster?"

Rooster was a stallion and older than Jackal, my eldest brother, who was two and thirty. Mouse gave a high-pitched mewl. It was her way of saying no.

"You had better wake him. The boys will be impatient to leave today. The snow is coming."

Mouse's response was a growl. I knew why she protested. Rooster was tired, but it could not be

4

helped. Even the old worked in Gnat, human and animal alike.

"I know he needs rest. If it were up to me, I would not send him into the forest at all."

Rooster accompanied my brothers on their hunt, and since we only had one stallion, they took turns riding him. Rooster was not fond of the woods and moved slowly. My brothers took this as being disobedient and whipped him to keep him moving. I hated it, but when I had voiced my anger, Jackal threatened to whip me. Rooster, sweet Rooster, had stepped between us, and his defiance had angered Jackal, but the threat of a strike from the powerful stallion kept him at bay.

"Strike me and I will put an arrow through your leg. I do not care if you are the only horse in all of Gnat," Jackal had threatened through clenched teeth. Then he looked at me. "And you. You will pay for his disobedience. Do you spend all your evenings in the barn whining about how terrible we are? No wonder he defies us. Well, I will show you cruel, you ungrateful git."

I spent the night in the barn after Jackal's threat, too afraid of what he might do in the night, but that had only delayed the inevitable. The next morning, he woke me by dousing me in ice-cold water and threw a dull knife at my feet.

"You will go to the moor and dig peat for our fires."

Still soaked, I had ventured into the bog. My fingers were so frozen, I could hardly hold the knife.

I would have never guessed that day, born in so much misery, would lead to an even worse day—the day I would eventually betray the fae man I loved.

You really are a silly git, I told myself. *You cannot love a man you have never really seen.*

But I knew by the way my chest ached, I had.

Thankfully, I was roused from the pain by a sharp cry from Mouse, a familiar sound that usually signaled the approach of one of my brothers. My heart raced as I whirled to see which of the three were approaching, except no one was there.

Still Mouse continued to hiss, showing her sharp teeth. The hair on her back stood on end.

I studied the tree line just beyond the rotting wooden fence that lined our property. The trees there were like giants—ancient and menacing. Thick fog poured from the darkness between the trunks, snaking through the air toward me like beckoning fingers. Though I saw nothing else, that did not mean no one was there. The fae usually moved about the world invisible to mortals. It was when they chose to show themselves that trouble followed, and while there was a part of me that wished I had never met the nameless, faceless fae, there was also a part of me that wondered—that wished, though those were dangerous things—that it was he who watched me so closely.

I shook my head to dismiss the thoughts and then reached for Mouse, who I held against my breast.

"Nothing to worry over, sweetling," I said, placing her on the ground. "Now go and rouse Rooster."

Mouse cut me a sharp look before stretching and wandering off to the barn.

I finished gathering the wood and returned to the cottage. With the kindling restocked and the fire lit and warming the house, I started breakfast, frying ham and potatoes, boiling eggs, and porridge. With everything prepared and warming, I headed upstairs to perform my most dreaded task—waking my brothers.

It did not matter that the three expected me every morning. I was always faced with some kind of threat. If they did not curse at me, they threw whatever was in reach. I'd already tried keeping their tables clear, except that night, each brother had brought every breakable thing to their bedside and threw it at me when I opened the door the next morning.

I decided then my attempts to make my life a little more bearable weren't worth the consequences. So my brothers did what they wanted to me, and so long as Mouse and Rooster were safe, I thought I could take it.

I topped the steps and approached the first door on the right. The room belonged to my youngest brother, Hans. He was the quietest of the three, and while that meant he did not subject me to quite as many insults, his preferred method of torture was what he called *tricks*.

The door creaked as it opened, and it was dark. The embers in his fireplace were nearly snuffed out. I glanced at the bed and could not see Hans, though that was usual. He liked to bury himself beneath the covers. That was probably best. It would be easier to revive the fire with him asleep.

I crossed to the hearth and kneeled, repeating the same process I'd gone through downstairs, except this time, the bucket of kindling was full. With the fire blazing, I started to rise when someone shoved me.

I flailed and caught myself, palms pressed flat against the hot stone of the hearth. The pain was instant and sharp. I yelped and pushed away, landing on my ass. For a few seconds, I could do nothing but sit in quiet shock, palms red and throbbing.

Behind me, Hans broke into peals of laughter.

"You should have known better than to assume I was asleep!"

My eyes watered, partly from the pain but also from embarrassment. I shoved those feelings down, because they had no place here. No one survived this life feeling sorry for themselves. Besides, Hans was right—I should have known.

I rose to my feet, pushing up from the cold stone floor, wincing at the pain. The palms of my hands felt taut, as if I suddenly didn't have enough skin.

I would have left without a word, but I thought the consequences might be worse if I did, so I spoke.

"It is good you are awake," I said, meeting his blue eyes. They were most like mine but untouched by burden or fear. "Breakfast will be ready soon."

His face turned pink, the color settling most in his cheeks.

"Aren't you going to laugh at my trick?" he asked.

I stared at him for a few seconds, knowing he wasn't joking, and then opened my mouth and laughed—or tried to. It was a hollow, joyless sound, but I had never truly laughed around my brother, so Hans would not know the difference.

Hans joined, laughing so loud, I could barely hear myself, and then he stopped abruptly, a cold mask descending over his face.

"Get the fuck out of my room," he said.

I left and moved to the next, which belonged to my middle brother, Michal. When I opened the door, I found a naked woman with long blond hair straddling him. They moved together, moaning. It was not the first time I'd gone to wake up my brother and found him like this, but it was the first time I'd seen Llywelyn, the chaplain's daughter, in his bed.

I walked farther into the room to tend to the fire. Llywelyn shrieked when she noticed me and reached for the blankets to cover her chest.

"What are you doing, you ugly little wench?" she snapped.

"Ignore her," Michal grunted.

"Ignore her? How am I supposed to ignore her? She is right there!"

"Think of her as a maid," he said.

"But she isn't a maid. She is your sister! What if she tells my father?"

"She will keep our secrets, or she will find herself in a grave."

Llywelyn giggled at Michal's threat, but it was not the first time he had made it. Truthfully, I did not care what my brothers did outside of hunting, and I only cared that they hunted so I could be alone.

When I was finished, I stood and turned to them. They were still kissing and rocking against each other. Michal's bed frame squeaked with each movement.

"Breakfast is soon," I said, adding as I headed for the door, "The church bells will ring in less than an hour."

I left Michal's room and made my way to my eldest brother's door, my heart pounding hard in my chest. Despite being used to Jackal's cruelty, my body always warned me away. But I knew if I ran, things would only be worse, so I entered his room.

It was dark, save for the hearth, where dying embers burned.

I crossed to the window and opened the curtains to let in the dreary morning light. Sometimes that was enough to rouse him, but not today. He remained on his side, eyes closed, dark hair mussed from sleep.

"Jackal," I whispered, afraid to startle him. "Jackal."

I spoke his name louder, noticing his eyes fluttering.

"It's time to wake up. Breakfast will be—"

Jackel's eyes flew open, and I stumbled back as he sat up and reached for the pitcher by his bed and threw it. I could feel it brush the edge of my clothes before it slammed against the wall. Pieces of ceramic and water exploded everywhere.

"You fucking ratbag!" he seethed.

His eyes were dark with rage. I had given up trying to figure out what had angered him. Sometimes, he just woke up like this.

"Get me another pitcher!" he ordered. "And clean this up!"

I obeyed, leaving to retrieve a new pitcher, though the only other one I had was my own. I filled it with water, gathered rags and a broom, and headed back upstairs.

Jackel waited, standing in his nightshirt. I started past him, intending to place the pitcher on his table again, but he stopped me.

"Give me the pitcher," he said.

So I did.

Then he poured the contents over my head.

"More water, wench," he said, shoving the pitcher into my hands.

There was nothing else to do but obey.

When I returned a second time, Jackal was dressed. He wore a dark woolen tunic over trousers and high boots. He looked like our father, with his proud, chiseled face and dark shorn hair. I hated it because my father had loved me, and Jackal did not.

He let me pass and return the pitcher to his bedside table. While he washed his face, I hurried to clear a path so that Jackal could leave his room without his boots getting wet or pieces of ceramic in his soles.

I worked fast and was finished by the time he turned and strolled out of his room, following at a distance as he headed to the kitchen. I would have to finish cleaning later. For now, I had to serve the hunters breakfast.

When I entered the kitchen, my brothers and a now-clothed Llywelyn sat around the long banquet table. It was far grander than any other piece of furniture in our cottage, because my father had made it, though over the years, the wood had worn, and if they weren't careful, they would end up with splinters in their fingers.

I worked in silence as I filled plates of food and tankards of beer for the boys and Llywelyn, who sat in Michal's lap.

"It is so dangerous to hunt in the Enchanted Forest!" said Llywelyn. "How do you manage to come out alive?"

It was the answer everyone in Gnat wanted. There were rumors, of course, that my brothers had been kissed by the fae or graced by witches, but I suspected something far more nefarious.

The fae were not kind, and neither were witches. Whatever gave my brothers the power to enter the forest unharmed was closer to a curse than anything.

"It is a skill," said Michal.

"I should like to watch you hunt," she said.

"No," Jackal snapped.

Llywelyn glared at him but was not deterred by my brother's rudeness.

"What will you hunt today?" she asked.

"Whatever crosses our path," Michal answered.

"I hope you will find a stag," she said, and then in a

low, sultry voice, she added, "It would keep me fed for a whole month."

"I will keep you fed," said Michal. "I will fill you up."

She giggled and leaned close as if to kiss him, but before their lips could touch, Hans spoke.

"Funny," he said. "I heard you say the same thing to the sheriff's daughter last week and the mayor's daughter the week before."

Both Michal and Llywelyn glared at him, but Llywelyn did not seem to care that Michal had more than one lover. She turned her attention to him, looping her arms around his neck.

"Perhaps you have promised them something, but you have promised me more."

A heavy silence followed her statement, and after a few seconds, Jackal stopped eating and set his fork and knife on the tabletop, his stare trained on the two lovers.

"Promises are dangerous," Jackal said. "You did not promise, did you, Michal?"

"N-no," Michal stammered. "Of course not."

"And why should he not promise?" Llywelyn demanded. "I have been a good lover. I have been a loyal lover."

"You are engaged to the sheriff's son," said Hans. "You are anything but loyal."

Llywelyn had nothing to say.

Jackal rose to his feet.

"Promises are binding, but they can be broken," said Jackal. "Lies do the breaking, Llywelyn. There are always consequences for lies."

Llywelyn straightened beneath my brother's threat but

said nothing. Jackal left the kitchen. Hans followed, and so did Michal, who shoved Llywelyn aside and stumbled after them, not sparing her a single glance. She sat, stunned, mouth open and eyes wide, realizing suddenly that she had chosen the wrong brother to seduce.

I grabbed my cloak and trailed behind my brothers, stopping at the door. Jackal had mounted Rooster, and Hans had hopped in the wood cart tethered to his harness. Since Michal was the last to join, he walked behind them as they made their way into the forest.

I watched them go and Llywelyn approached, pausing to look at me.

"Why do you stay here?" she asked. "You could leave while they are away."

Her question felt like a trap, a way to trick me into saying something she could offer to my eldest brother.

"I belong here," I answered.

Llywelyn gave a breathless laugh. "I thought there were consequences to lies, Samara."

I looked at the woman, fair even in the pale morning light. It might be a lie, but for me, the truth always had greater consequences. It was something she would never understand.

"The church bells are ringing," I said, and as the words left my mouth, a silver sound echoed in the faraway distance.

Llewelyn's eyes grew wide and her cheeks red. "You cruel wench! You were supposed to warn me!"

She shoved past me, my shoulder slamming into the frame of the door as she sprinted across the frozen ground, down the winding road, and into the town of Gnat.

CHAPTER TWO
A Handsome Prince

SAMARA

I watched my brothers until they were consumed by the forest, and for a brief moment, I found myself hoping they never returned, but my guilt was so great, I spoke aloud to whoever might have heard my thoughts.

"Forgive me. I know not what I think," I said.

It would be better if I disappeared. I had nothing to offer Gnat, save what I did for my brothers, but there were a number of women, as Michal so often demonstrated, willing to fill my role, and they would do so happily.

Even knowing that, I did not leave. I couldn't. Llywelyn was wrong. This house belonged to my parents. My father had built it, and my mother had made it beautiful with her paintings. They were buried in this ground. I could not leave them, and I could not leave Mouse or Rooster. They were my best friends, and I would never abandon them to the cruelty of my brothers no matter how often I dreamed of a different life—or none at all.

I closed the door and headed back to the kitchen where I gathered the dishes, sliding scraps into a bucket. I'd have to bury them later, since I could not be sure that Hans hadn't poisoned what remained. I had only made that mistake once—tossing leftovers out the back, thinking that the birds or the deer might eat them, but the next morning, I'd found three dead wolves.

Hans had laughed—and then laughed harder when I'd had to bury them.

Once the dishes were washed, I moved upstairs to finish cleaning Jackal's floor.

I lowered to my hands and knees, prying pieces of ceramic from between the cracks of the wooden floor with a knife. I suspected my brother had crushed them into the seams when I'd gone downstairs for another pitcher, and I knew if he found so much as a sliver of porcelain remaining, he'd break everything in the house in retaliation.

So I was careful, but the pieces were sharp and cut into my fingers. I did not mind the pain so much as the blood, because it reminded me of my dream, and my dream reminded me of the fae, and the fae reminded me that I had once been in love.

Foolishly in love.

And when I thought about love, I thought of everything that came with it and what I would never have— passion, protection, trust. I'd longed for someone to touch me because they desired me, and I'd wished for it only once. In the aftermath of that wish, whatever magic hung heavy in the air forced me to cut off the only hand that had offered me any kindness.

When I was certain there was not a single shard of ceramic left, I scrubbed Jackal's floor on my hands and knees and moved on to Michal's and Hans's rooms, then the staircase and the small living room, where I had to pause because the floor was covered in what appeared to be black soot—ashes from the fireplace.

Another one of Hans's cruel jokes.

My face was suddenly flooded with heat, and my fingers curled into my palms. I was used to this feeling— this deep and painful anger—but this time, it frightened me because I couldn't shove it down. Instead, I let it erupt and used it as I dragged the ash-covered rug outside and heaved it over the rotting wooden fence. I swiped a log from the ground and began to beat the rug.

Plumes of dust blinded and choked me, and my fingers slipped on the loose bark, but I couldn't stop, and I didn't until the fence collapsed.

My chest ached with each panting breath as I staggered back, dropping the log at my feet. I screamed until my anger was gone and I had no strength left to stand. I fell to my knees, my throat raw, tears burning my eyes. The rage that had fed me turned to panic.

"No, no, no."

I got to my feet and moved the rug, which had fallen into the mud. It was ruined, and so was the fence. Two posts were broken, and the rotting rails that ran between them were shattered.

If my brothers came home and saw the fence broken, the punishment would be severe—likely a beating with the very log I used to destroy it.

How could I be so stupid!

I looked toward the Enchanted Forest, wondering how long until my brothers returned. Could I repair the fence in time? My eyes shifted to the pile of wood by the barn. Or could I hide it?

Something furry brushed my ankle.

"You wouldn't happen to know where I could find some wood, Mouse?"

She paused, looked up at me, and meowed, then took off, trotting toward the side of the house. I followed as she rounded the corner and found her sitting beside a pile of wood, but it was not wood for the fence. It was the kindling I'd gathered for the fire, and it lay beneath my eldest brother's window.

I thought I'd been pushed to my breaking point already, except now I knew otherwise.

This was my breaking point.

But it didn't feel like I had expected. It was not the anger that had stolen my sanity moments ago. This wasn't even emotion—it was a lack of it. I was no longer worried about what would happen if my brothers returned to find the fence broken or the rug destroyed, because neither of those things mattered, especially because I would not be here for them to punish.

I turned and walked down the sloping hill behind our cottage. At the very bottom, two rounded rocks marked where my mother and father lay. I continued past them, knowing if I stopped, I would succumb to the guilt that had kept me obedient.

I followed a worn and familiar trail through the woods. These were not the same ominous trees and dark pines of the Enchanted Forest. There was a creek at the bottom, and I followed it as it twisted and turned through more rolling hills, all covered in decaying leaves and pine needles. I walked until my calves hurt and my feet ached. I could tell when I was near my destination because the sky seemed to open up before me, and as I came to the cliff's edge, it was truly endless. The clouds hung heavy and low, casting large shadows over the rocky valley below. That was my destination, where the earth would cradle my body, eat my flesh, and consume my bones.

I thought that sounded beautiful. Peaceful even.

I desired anything but what lay behind me.

Sand and stones tumbled over the cliff as I inched closer, until the tips of my toes hung over the edge. A wave of dizziness rushed to my head, and my legs shook. I should have closed my eyes, but I didn't. Instead, I spread my arms wide, letting the cold wind wash over me, and as I did, it began to snow.

"Are you going to kill yourself?"

The sudden sound of a strange voice drew my attention. I turned my head to find a man standing near. He was handsome with large blue eyes and dark hair, but he was almost too pretty. His skin was unmarred by sun or scars, and his lips were full and pillowy, not cracked and dry. He wore a heavy wool cloak, and though it concealed what he wore beneath, I suspected his sleeves were threaded with gold. He held a hat against his chest. A long red feather was stuck in the band.

I looked away and answered, "I have not decided."

"It would be a shame," he said.

I thought I could feel him draw nearer.

"You are too beautiful to die."

"That is a foolish thing to say," I said. "Death does not care about beauty."

If he had, he would not have taken my mother or my father.

He would have taken my brothers.

"Every man cares about beauty," he replied.

"You believe death is a man?"

"Do you think a woman can take a life?" he returned.

"Yes," I said, meeting his gaze. "At the very least, I could take my own."

"Why do I get the feeling you would just to prove me wrong?"

"You are vain, my lord," I said. "This is not about you at all. Now if you would kindly leave me to my death."

"I couldn't possibly leave now that I know your intentions."

"Why not? Do you want to watch?"

"No, I hope to change your mind."

"You won't," I said. "I have decided."

"Truly?"

"Yes."

"Then why haven't you jumped?"

"Because you have interrupted my concentration."

"Ending your life doesn't sound like something that needs concentration."

"So you have tried before?"

"Well, no."

"Then how would you know?"

"By deduction," he replied. "Hard things require concentration. Jumping off a cliff isn't hard."

"I suppose that depends on your definition of hard. The ground is quite solid."

The man chuckled, and there was a glint in his eyes I had never seen in anyone else's, but that was because this man was not burdened with the worry of surviving. He probably carried a silver spoon in his pocket, and while he had likely used it all his life, it had not given him a silver tongue.

"You are quite clever," he said.

"Too clever to die?" I asked.

"No one is too clever to die," the man replied.

"Once again, you speak for death," I said. "Worse, you believe he values beauty over genius."

"Beauty is genius," said the man. "Surely, it sways you."

"Sways? No," I said. "I have met many beautiful, terrible people."

"I suppose I have too," he said and then paused. "So what is it, then, that you value?"

"Kindness," I said.

I expected the lord to laugh, but he didn't, and when I looked at him, his eyes had changed.

"Has anyone ever been kind to you?"

I looked away. I could not face his pity.

"A long time ago."

"Have I been kind to you?"

"I hardly know you," I said.

"Would you give me time to show you I can be kind?"

"We will not see each other again beyond this moment," I said.

"Because you intend to die?"

"Yes," I said. "But even if I lived."

He paused for a moment, inching closer. I considered

what I would do if he reached for me. Would I jump to spite him, or let him pull me close?

"Would you be treated poorly if I saw you again?"

I did not answer.

"What if I took you from this place?"

I was surprised by the sound that came out of my mouth—a guttural laugh.

"I could not leave even if I wanted to."

"Why not?"

"Because—" I started, but when I could think of no reason, I paused. "Just because."

"I would keep you safe," he said.

"I do not even know that word," I said. "And I do not know you."

He held my gaze with those beautiful blue eyes. They were startling, and while I had never seen the eyes of the fae I had yearned for the last seven years, they reminded me that I had once dreamed of meeting his gaze and discovering his eyes were the same icy shade.

The man extended his hand.

I did not take it, but he waited.

Finally, I relented, startled by how soft his fingers were, and I immediately felt flushed, aware of how rough my own were.

"I am Prince Henry from the Kingdom of Rook," he said and pressed his lips to my red and swollen knuckles. Then he lifted his gaze to mine and smiled. "Now we are not strangers."

"Your name does not make us anything more than acquaintances," I said.

"Usually when one offers a name, the courteous thing to do is give yours," he said.

22

"You must do this often then," I said.

"Meet strange girls in the woods who want to end their life? No," he said. "I must admit, this is a first for me."

I tried not to smile at him.

I didn't *want* to smile at him.

"Samara," I said.

"Samara," he repeated, grinning. "Was that so hard?"

"Terribly," I replied.

"Samara," he said again. "Let me take you away from this horrible place."

I shook my head. "And trade my situation for what? Something far worse? Never."

"I do not think becoming my wife would be worse."

"Your *wife*?"

"Marry me," he said.

"You are delusional," I said.

"I am not."

"You just met me. I'm a strange girl in the woods, remember?"

"Yes, and you are very enchanting."

"Did you eat mushrooms?"

He opened his mouth but hesitated. "That's not the point. The point is I would like to offer you a better life."

"There are other ways to do that than marriage."

"If you will not marry me, then come away with me to Rook. I can give you a better life, and perhaps, after some time, you will agree to be my wife."

"Why? Why would you want to rescue me?"

"Because despite what you believe, there are kind people in the world, Samara."

I stared at this man—this strange man who had found me in the woods.

"You will have to ask my brothers," I said. "It will not be easy."

"Am I correct that it isn't because they love you dearly?"

"If that were the case, you would not have convinced me with so little effort."

"You call that little effort?" he asked, though his eyes sparkled with mirth. "I practically had to beg."

"I'm sure it must have been difficult for you to be told no," I said. "First time?"

He chuckled. "Unfortunately no," he said and then grew a little more serious. "I know you must think poorly of me given my title, but I intend to show you we are not all so terrible."

"It is just like a prince to presume to know my mind," I said, but the statement had no power behind it, because the prince was right—I did not have a high opinion of him or any who ruled by right of blood.

Henry smiled. "Do not worry about your brothers," he said, tugging on my hand. "I will make them an offer they cannot refuse."

I allowed him to lead me away from the cliff, down the balding path and into the woods where a beautiful horse waited. I had never seen one with such a coat and mane—white with black spots.

"Oh, he is beautiful," I said.

"Thank you," Henry replied, taking the reins. "Her name is River."

"Oh," I said, blushing. "I'm sorry."

"Do not worry. She is not offended," he said. "Come, I will help you up."

"I do not need help," I said.

I knew how to ride a horse.

I put my left foot in the stirrup and held the pommel as I swung my right foot over, sinking into the saddle with ease. When I met the prince's gaze, his cheeks were tinged with pink.

"You," he said and then cleared his throat. "You do not want to sit sidesaddle?"

"No. Why would I?"

He rubbed the back of his head. The redness had spread to his ears.

"Well, you are in a gown," he said. "And riding astride shows your...legs."

"My legs?" I looked down, seeing that my dress had ridden up to the tops of my knees. I hadn't noticed it because I was used to it, but suddenly I realized why the prince was so embarrassed.

"Haven't you ever seen a woman's legs before?" I asked.

"Well, yes, but—"

"But mine make you nervous?"

"Not nervous," he said.

"So they offend you?"

"No, of course not," he stammered. "They are very nice legs. You...have very nice legs."

I stared at him, smirking.

"Forget I said anything at all," he said, putting on his hat.

"I will never," I said, as he mounted River, but my amusement died as soon as he was seated behind me.

I had never been so close to a man before, never felt another body against my own like this. He was warm, and as he reached past me to take the reins, I felt like I could sense his strength in the hard muscles of his chest and arms. It was the first time I found myself thinking about what was beneath the finery of his clothing.

Suddenly, I was the one blushing.

"Ready?" he asked.

I went rigid when I felt his breath on my ear, and all I could do was nod, humiliated by my sinful thoughts.

He chuckled as he tugged on the reins. I didn't dare ask him what was so funny, because I knew that if he tried to guess my thoughts this time, he would finally be right.

I did not speak beyond offering the prince directions to the cottage, too focused on every part of my body that touched him. It was an odd feeling, to be so close to a stranger. I found myself studying his hands as he held the reins before me. They were...normal. Not overly large but graceful. His nails were trimmed short and clean, and he had no cuts or scars.

A strange disappointment blossomed in my stomach.

"Do you have a sword?" I asked.

"Why? Already planning my demise?" he asked.

"I just wondered if you used it," I said.

"When the occasion calls for it," he said. "Why?"

"Because...your hands are soft."

"You think my hands are soft?"

"It isn't a thought," I said. "I know."

The prince was quiet for a moment.

"You have a strange way of making me feel very insecure," he said.

"It was only an observation," I said.

He lifted his hand, and I could not help but flinch. He quickly lowered it again.

"I won't hurt you," he said, his voice gentle, yet I did not believe him.

"So you say."

"I will prove it in time," he said.

There was a part of me that wanted to hope he was honorable and would keep his word, but I had already let myself hope once, and it had only led to disappointment.

"You may not want to after you meet my brothers."

We were silent after that, and I found myself worrying over what my brothers would say when they arrived home to find a handsome prince asking for my hand in marriage. I was certain they would not expect it, because they did not think it possible that anyone could ever want me. I was not even sure this was real. Maybe it was just one of Hans's cruel pranks.

Why would a prince of Rook be wandering through the woods in Gnat alone? The longer I thought, the more suspicious I grew, and my body responded in kind. I straightened my back and leaned forward, attempting to put as much distance between me and the prince as I could, though the horse did not allow for much, and the prince only tightened his hold around my waist.

"Do not be afraid," he said.

"I don't know how," I said.

"You do not know how?" he repeated.

"I have only ever been afraid," I said.

Again Henry did not speak, and I was certain he did not know what to do with me.

Once we came to the creek, the prince led River along the bank, up and down every hill, past my mother's and father's graves, to the doorstep of my weathered cottage where my three brothers waited. They each carried a weapon—Hans an axe, Michal a bow, and Jackal a sword.

"What is the meaning of this?" asked Michal.

The prince dismounted and then held his hand out for me. I did not take it and instead slipped off River's back and put distance between him, myself, and my brothers.

"Good sirs," he said, taking off his feathered hat and holding it to his breast. "I am Prince Henry of the Kingdom of Rook. I happened upon your sister in the wood, and I would like to have her to wife. What say you?"

There was a long pause, and Hans was the first to laugh, followed by Michal, but what scared me the most was that Jackal had yet to speak or even blink.

"You want to marry our sister?" Hans asked, still laughing. "You'd be better off marrying a pig!"

"Aye," said Michal. "And a pig is prettier."

"I am certain we are not speaking of the same woman," said the prince, whose voice was stern.

"He has been bespelled!" said Michal.

"Enchanted, I assure you," said the prince.

"Prince," said Hans. "You have looked upon the fae, and they have given you false eyes!"

"I have gazed upon no fae," said the prince. "I have only the assurance that I have met my future wife, your sister. I will ask once again for her hand in marriage."

There was a quiet pause after the prince finished speaking.

Michal shook his head in disbelief. "Are you hearing this, Jackal?"

It wasn't until I heard my eldest brother's name that

I looked up, catching his cold stare before he turned his attention to the prince, angling his head so that he appeared curious.

"Tell me, Prince," said Jackal. "What do you want in a wife?"

The prince hesitated. "I suppose I have not given it much thought."

"How can you want my sister to wife if you don't even know what you want?"

"Because I can see her," replied the prince.

"So this is about fucking," said Michal. "If that is the case, there is the barn."

"Are you suggesting I am dishonorable?"

"No, Prince, but you are a man," said Michal.

"A man, perhaps, but I would never dishonor a woman in such a way, especially one I intend to marry. Now, I will ask for your blessing a final time. Allow me your sister's hand in marriage, and you will be rewarded handsomely."

There was silence.

"Handsomely, you say?" asked Jackal. "What have you to offer in exchange for our dear, dear sister?"

"I will bring you three treasures from my father's vault. A golden ring, a singing lark, and an enchanted rose."

"What use would we, three starving hunters, have for a ring, a bird, and a rose?"

"Then I shall bring you gold and silver," Henry said. "And everything else I have named shall go to your sister."

"Bring us gold and silver," said Jackal. "And you can have our sister as a wife."

"Do I have your word?"

"You have my word," said Jackal. "We shall wait for

your arrival at sunrise—and not a moment past or our agreement is forfeit."

The prince turned to me, and my eyes widened.

"I will think of nothing but you until we are reunited at dawn."

He glanced at my brothers before he secured his hat, mounted his horse, and rode off, feather bouncing as he went.

"Do you think he'll be back?" asked Hans.

Michal scoffed. "Not a chance. He will return to his golden castle on his golden hill and forget she ever existed."

It was something I did not doubt.

Jackal shoved past Michal and Hans as he came for me. I stumbled back and fell to the ground at his approach.

"What do you think you are doing?" he snarled, looming over me with hate-filled eyes.

"N-nothing," I said. "I didn't do anything!"

He grabbed me by my hair and dragged me to my feet, but I had grown so used to the feeling, I didn't even cry out. I just followed as he pulled.

"Did you seduce him?" he demanded.

"No! I would never!"

I didn't know how.

"Liar!" he accused. "You fucked him, didn't you?"

"I swear I didn't!" I said. "I swear upon the graves of our parents!"

His grip tightened, and he leaned closer to me, his eyes full of such hate, I could feel the heat of it burning me from the inside out.

"If I so much as sense a baby in your belly, I will slice

you open and tear it out," he said, and then he shoved his knee into my stomach, and I felt a burst of pain and nausea all at once.

He released me, and I fell to the ground, curling into myself as he landed another blow to my stomach before Michal grabbed his arm and pulled him back.

"Stop, Jackal!" he said. "What if you kill her and the prince returns?"

"If the prince returns, then he can carry away her corpse," he said.

"Aye, he may, but will he pay?" said Michal. "Besides, it is nearing sundown, and I am starved. Who will cook for us if she is dead?"

I was so consumed trying to breathe through the pain, I didn't know if Michal's words had swayed my brother, but in some ways, I didn't care. If this was to be my end, at least eventually, there would be no pain.

"Get up!" Jackal commanded suddenly, and I peeled open my eyes to find all three brothers standing over me.

I held my stomach tightly, fighting the nausea as I got to my feet.

"Feed us, wash the rug, fix the fence, and do not dream of sleep until you are certain you are done, or I will have you dancing to your death in iron-hot shoes."

Jackal turned and entered the house. Michal offered me a strange look—not pity but interest. He'd never considered the possibility that I might bring them wealth. Hans spit in my face before he turned to leave, laughing maniacally as he headed into the house.

Once they were inside, I bent at the waist and vomited all over my feet.

CHAPTER THREE
The Fox and the Fae

SAMARA

I continued to feel nauseous throughout the evening and night. My stomach felt heavy; the ache was constant. I wondered as I worked to feed my brothers, clean the rug, and fix the fence if I would die by morning. Despite the pain, I smiled at the thought that my brothers would forfeit their payment of gold and silver. I wondered if this was what it felt like to have power, however little.

It was dark when I finished the fence, and I was frozen to the bone. I looked up at the sky, knowing I would see nothing but a dark void. The air was heavy with the smell of snow, crisp and crystalline. I took a deep breath, filling my lungs with it. The cold felt good despite the sharp twist in my gut, and my breath clouded the air as I exhaled. I looked toward the barn where Rooster and Mouse were likely asleep and considered staying there on my final night at home, but instead, I gathered my lantern and cloak close and walked toward Daft Moor.

The night was still as I took the familiar, winding path to the bog. I had once found such comfort in this short stroll. Now all I felt was dread, but it seemed important to say goodbye, whether I died or left with the prince tomorrow.

As I neared, my heart began to race, and something thick gathered in my throat. I was frustrated by these emotions, still just as fresh and violent as they were seven years ago. I knew the feelings would cease with death, but would they with distance? Time surely had not helped.

The path dipped down into a valley with great boulders on either side, covered in browning moss. It was here I first met the fae who had offered his hand and the knife that had changed my life. I paused on the edge of the moor. I paused on the edge of the moor where, the rich scent of dark earth reached me. It held so many memories, both terrible and thrilling. I could not decide how to feel, though I didn't know why. This place had been a source of misery, yet I felt a pang of sadness leaving. There were things here I still loved—the house my father built, their bodies in their graves, the animals both wild and tamed, even the fae who had given me the knife, as ridiculous as it was—but now it was time to let those things go. They were anchors to a past that kept me a breath from the surface, drowning beneath the weight of things that were nothing but dreams.

"I had never felt such hope as I did when you came to my aid until today," I said. "I can finally let you go."

The lie tasted bitter in my mouth, but if I said it

enough, maybe it would be true. I took one final breath of cold, rich air and turned to leave when I caught sight of two glowing eyes. I gasped and stepped back, tripping on a boulder, falling against it.

The creature blinked at me twice and then slipped out from where it hid between two large stones—the same stones from which the fae had offered the knife.

It was a fox, a beautiful fox with orange fur and white and black paws. He shook his head, large ears flip-flopping before he sat, curling his fluffy tail around his feet, and stared at me.

"I did not mean to startle you," he said.

It was my turn to blink. "Did you—"

"Talk?" he asked. "Yes."

I pressed my palms to my face. "I must be dead."

The fox's beady eyes narrowed.

"Not yet, though you soon will be. Let me lick your hand, and you shall be healed."

I hesitated.

"Trust me, wild one. I am here to help."

"Why?" I asked.

"I must," he answered but did not explain.

I offered my hand and felt the rough brush of the fox's tongue against my skin once, twice, three times before the pain in my stomach eased instantly. I pulled my hand back, examining the spot the fox had touched, but there was nothing. Then I pressed my hand to my stomach. It was no longer tender.

"You healed me," I said in quiet wonder.

"I would not lie," said the fox.

"Would not or could not?" I asked. The fox tilted his head as if he did not understand the question, so I asked,

"Are you fae?"

Fae could not lie—it was not a choice.

The fox bristled his tail as if he did not like that question.

"I am a fox," he said.

"I have never met a fox who could talk."

"I am a fox who can talk."

We were both quiet, staring at each other, and then a wave of guilt made my skin feel flushed.

"I'm sorry," I said. "Thank you for healing me."

"Do not thank me," he said. "Do as I say."

I frowned at his words, but he continued quickly.

"Tomorrow, the prince will arrive to take you away to his kingdom, but your carriage will be set upon by thieves. You must not move or make a sound, or they will kill you first. Wait, and you will be rescued."

"How do you know this?"

"I am a fox," he said.

"That hardly explains anything."

"It explains everything," he said.

"If this is true—"

"I would not lie," the fox reminded.

"Then perhaps I should not leave at all."

"You must," said the fox. "It has already been decided."

I did not know what to say, but the fox rose to his feet.

"Do not forget what I have said, or tomorrow, you will be dead."

Then he turned, tail swaying, and vanished into the dark between the stones. I stood there, staring, wondering what world I might find if I followed him.

Something cold touched my arm. When I looked, I saw snow melting on my skin. I lifted the lantern as icy crystals fell across the moor. The sound was silvery, beautiful like the laughter of the fae. It made me want to linger, and I did until the ground was covered with a thin layer of white I might have stayed there forever, under the spell of this magic until the blood froze in my veins, but a voice in the back of my mind was louder.

"Come away, Samara," it said. "There is nothing for you here but death."

I did not know who spoke, if it was my consciousness or the voice that called to me in my dreams, but it drew me away from the moor toward home.

The cottage was quiet and dark, save for the kitchen where the light from the hearth ignited the window, warm and welcoming. Anyone who passed would think it a quaint refuge from the cold, but it had been a long time since I'd felt safe beneath its roof. Instead of going inside to sleep, I made my way to the barn and rolled open the door, closing it quickly behind me.

When I turned, I found Rooster lying on a bed of hay. Mouse was curled up beside him sleeping. Rooster lifted his head and made a quiet, breathy sound as I approached.

I smiled and set the lantern down away from the hay.

"Hello, sweetling," I said, offering my hand, which he nuzzled before I caressed the space between his eyes, which fell closed. "It is good to see you. How was your day?"

He looked at me and then snorted as if to say *how do you think*?

"I know," I said. "My brothers are not the easiest to get along with."

Rooster blew out a harsh breath.

"I will take you from them someday," I said, pulling away. I sat beside Mouse and hauled her into my lap. She woke briefly, to meow and yawn, and then curled into a ball to sleep again as I rested my back against Rooster's flank.

This was the safest I had felt in a long while, though

I could not escape the guilt, knowing what tomorrow would bring. At dawn, the prince would arrive, and I would leave Rooster and Mouse behind. My stomach churned. I should have asked for more from the prince, but that decision likely would have proven fatal for my two friends. I did not doubt my brothers' ability to kill the two creatures I loved most in the world as retribution for my newfound freedom.

It would be safer to come for them after I left—if I left at all.

There was still a part of me that doubted Henry's return.

"Rooster, I have to tell you something," I said. "A prince has offered for my hand. He says he will come soon to collect me, not a moment before sunrise. I do not want to leave you—"

Rooster interrupted, making a sound deep in his throat and throwing his head back.

"I know it is a chance at a different life," I said. I did not want to say a *better* life, because I did not truly know that. "But I will never forgive myself if they harm you while I am away."

Rooster's neigh was quiet and deep, as if to say *do not worry about me*, but I would until I saw him again. I could not help feeling I was abandoning them to the cruelty of my brothers.

"I will ask the prince to send for you as soon as I am able," I promised.

He nuzzled my hair, and my eyes grew heavy, surrounded by their warmth. Finally, I fell into a deep sleep, unhindered by the haunting voice that had lulled me into slumber the last seven years.

I was roused by Mouse, who rubbed her head against my hand, purring loudly.

"What is it?" I asked, still half-asleep.

Rooster neighed deeply, and I had no choice but to get to my feet as he rolled to rise. I rubbed my eyes and realized why they were so alert—someone was coming. I could hear the rhythmic clop of hooves, and suddenly, my heart was pounding. I went to the door and pushed it open. It was still dark, but a faint orange light burned on the horizon. It reached far enough to glint off an approaching golden carriage pulled by four black horses.

My prince had come.

I watched as the coachman made a wide circle and came to a stop before my small, ruined cottage, now covered in fresh snow. Two footmen stepped down from the back, each dressed in regally cut coats the color of midnight and trimmed in glinting gold. One opened the door while the other pulled down a set of gilded steps, and then the prince emerged, dressed far more finely than he had been the day before. His surcoat glittered as the morning sun sliced across the yard, and his cloak was lined with fur as white as the snow on the ground. His eyes gleamed when he saw me, and he reached for my hand.

"Samara," he said, pressing his lips to my knuckles.

I could not help it. The corners of my lips lifted.

"Prince," I breathed.

His fingers tightened around mine, but a sharp sound drew our attention from each other to the door of the cottage where my three brothers stood.

"We had a deal, Prince," said Jackal.

Henry released my hand and stepped in front me as if to shield me from their sight.

"And I have honored it," said the prince.

Just then, the footmen rounded the carriage, heaving a massive chest that they dropped halfway between us and my brothers before opening it to reveal a towering pile of gold and silver. Michal's and Hans's eyes sparkled, but Jackal seemed unaffected by his new wealth, his hateful gaze boring into mine.

"Well?" Henry demanded.

Finally, Jackal's attention shifted to the prince. "I expect you will welcome us to your castle. We would very much like to visit our dear sister."

"Of course," said the prince, though tightly. "You shall be guests of honor at our wedding."

For a moment, no one spoke, and then the prince took a step back so that he stood beside me.

Even he did not trust my brothers enough to give them his back.

"Say your farewells, my darling," said Henry. "We are running late."

I did not move, only stared at my siblings, who had made my entire life up until this point completely miserable.

"Farewell," I said, but then I turned to Rooster and Mouse, who lingered in the doorway of the barn, and went to them. I scooped Mouse into my arms and held her close as I hugged Rooster's neck and whispered to them both. "I will return for you soon."

"Darling," the prince said.

Pressure built behind my eyes, but I refused to cry.

I turned toward the prince and met him at the carriage door.

"Do not fret," he said. "The misery ends today."

He took my hand and helped me into the carriage, and as I sank into the seat, I was surrounded by rich, red velvet. I had never seen such expensive fabrics or felt anything so soft. I clasped my hands between my thighs to keep from touching everything around me.

The prince sat across from me. He was so tall, our knees touched.

"Tell me now before we depart, did your brothers harm you in the night?"

I held his pretty, blue-eyed gaze and answered, "No, my lord."

It was an easy lie, because I had told it so often.

The prince stared at me, and I knew he did not believe me, but he also did not argue. He rapped on the ceiling, and I was jolted as the carriage surged forward. I stared out the large windows, watching my brothers as we passed, eyes connecting with Jackal's long enough that the coldness of his gaze froze my very blood. If he could have killed me then, he would have.

I turned my head away to look out the other window, spotting Rooster and Mouse watching our retreat, and pressed my hand to the window.

"I can send for your animals," said the prince.

I met his gaze.

"My brothers will demand a trade."

"Of course," said the prince. "I shall make the exchange tomorrow. Three fine stallions and seven feral cats for your one. Will that please you?"

I smiled at the thought of the prince unleashing seven feral cats on my brothers.

"I have never been asked that before," I said.

The prince smirked. "I shall ask it often."

A flush unfurled in my chest, warming my throat and face. I dropped my gaze to my hands, still clasped between my legs.

"Well?" asked the prince, and I looked at him. "You did not answer. Will that please you?"

I was quiet for a moment and then answered in a whisper, "Yes."

He grinned and seemed to relax.

We rode in silence for a few minutes as the carriage bounced along the winding snow-covered path. I kept my eyes focused outside, on the ominous tree line of the Enchanted Forest, near which we were currently traveling. I wondered how long we would be within her shadow.

"You look troubled," said the prince.

"I am only thinking of the forest," I said. "Do the fae go as far as Rook?"

"No village is safe from the creatures who reside within the Enchanted Forest," he said. His eyes darkened as he spoke, and his mouth tightened. "Their magic is strong, and their presence is a plague."

"You are angry," I said, voice quiet. I could not help the hint of fear that rattled my spine.

"Not at you," he said quickly. "Oh my dear, not at you. My kingdom has long been at war with the forest, for you see, my sister was taken by the fae, and in her place, they left such an awful child. A changeling so cruel she has been imprisoned within her room until the true princess can be found."

"How terrible," I said. "I am so sorry."

The prince offered a small smile.

"Stop apologizing for things you did not do."

I started to open my mouth, but the only thing on the tip of my tongue was an apology, so I decided to change the subject.

"What will happen once we arrive at the castle?"

"You will be taken to your rooms, where your ladies-in-waiting will bathe and dress you, and then I shall present you to my father and mother, and we will feast with the court to celebrate our engagement," he said. "Tomorrow, we shall marry."

The shock of his words hit my chest, making me sit straighter.

"You said we could wait to wed until I was ready."

"My darling, it is hardly appropriate for me to take you from your family and not marry you quickly, and I cannot leave you at the castle unwed while I am gone."

"Gone?" I repeated, another wave of surprise striking deep in the pit of my stomach.

"I take no pleasure in leaving you so soon after the wedding, of course," he said. "If I could delay it, I would, but you must understand, when I stumbled upon you in the forest yesterday, I was in search of my brother."

"You have a brother too?"

"I have two," he said. "But one went in search of a tree with golden apples somewhere within the Enchanted Forest and has not returned."

I sat quietly for a few moments, my emotions warring. I did not know what to think of the information the prince had just chosen to impart to me. I did not know how to feel about marrying him so soon and then being left alone. What if his mother and father were not so kind?

"Why did your brother go in search of a golden apple?"

"He wished to marry his beloved," he said. "But her father, the king of Holle, has demanded a golden apple in exchange for her hand. Of course, my brave brother was more than willing."

"If your brother has not returned, will you?" I asked.

He tilted his chin down and leaned forward, lowering his voice as he spoke. "I will, so long as I know you are waiting for me."

His words made my chest ache, and I swallowed hard as a strange tension filled the space between us. I wanted to look away to regain my composure, but I couldn't.

"Samara." He said my name, warm and breathless, then his eyes fell to my lips, and I was spellbound as I waited for him to kiss me, but then the carriage came to a hard stop, and I was thrown forward into his arms.

Outside the carriage, there came a thud, a scream, and then a shout.

"Run, Your Highness!"

I felt an overwhelming burst of fear. It was sudden and hot and made my heart race. I pushed away from the prince, meeting his gaze. He did not appear to be afraid but angry, his mouth tense. Suddenly, I remembered the fox's warning from last night—*Tomorrow, your carriage will be set upon by thieves. You must not move or make a sound, or they will kill you. Wait, and you will be rescued.*

The memory was hazy, as if it had been a dream, but here it was happening.

I started to speak, to tell the prince what the fox had said, but before I could, the carriage door flew open, and the prince spoke. "Take what you want, but do not harm—"

His words were cut short, and I found myself splattered with something wet. I blinked, temporarily blinded by it, and wiped my eyes, only to see red stain my fingers.

Blood.

I looked up to see that the prince was dead, an arrow embedded in his eye socket. He fell back against the seat limply.

My mouth opened in silent horror as panic flooded my body.

I wanted to scream as fear clawed at my chest, but I could only think of the fox's words, so I stayed silent and still, even as the thief pulled me from the carriage by my ankles to the ground, where I hit hard, head ricocheting off the earth.

I bit down on my tongue as pain exploded behind my eyes, and still I did not move, even as the thief strad-dled me. I expected him to do something terrible, but he only frowned as he stared down at me. He was a grisly-looking man, large with dark, stringy hair and a wild, unkempt beard.

"Oi! What is it, Peter?" a voice shouted.

"Oi, Arthur!" said Peter. "This girl, she is as still and silent as a statue!"

"Oi!" said another voice. "Perhaps she is dead."

Peter stared down at me. "I don't know, Puck. Her eyes are open."

"People die with their eyes open!" he argued.

Peter put his ear to my chest. I was repulsed by his sour smell and where we touched. Everything inside me was desperate to shove him off, yet I remained still, as if the fox's words were magic and froze my limbs.

After a few seconds, Peter straightened. "No, her heart is beating!"

"Maybe she is mute!" Arthur called.

"Are you mute?" Peter asked.

I did not move, not even to shake my head.

"She isn't answering!" Peter said over his shoulder.

"Perhaps she cannot hear you," said Puck.

Peter looked down at me and then yelled. "Can you hear me?"

I just stared at him.

"Oi, you idiot!" Arthur said. This time when he spoke, he sounded closer. "If she cannot hear, she will not understand you!"

"How do you know?" asked Peter. "She might read lips."

After a few seconds, the man I presumed was Arthur came into view. He was equally as repulsive, but his hair was shorter, and he had a mustache that was so long, it curled into his mouth. Then another joined. This must be Puck, the third thief. His hair was red and stood on end, and while he was clean-shaven, I suspected it was because he could not grow a beard.

"Where did she come from?" asked Puck.

"I pulled her from the carriage," said Peter.

"She was with the prince?" asked Arthur, as if he did not believe it could be true.

"Oi, I *just* said that," said Peter.

"She does not look like royalty," said Arthur, scanning my clothes.

"Perhaps she is his whore," said Puck.

"She doesn't seem afraid," observed Peter.

"That has nothing to do with being a whore," said Puck.

"No, but I don't like it," said Peter.

"Nor do I," said Arthur.

Then they all shivered violently.

"Did you feel that?" asked Arthur.

"I did," said Puck. "What was it?"

"I believe it was…a…shiver," said Peter.

"A shiver?" Arthur question.

"Surely not!" said Puck.

"We would never fear such a frail thing—and a woman at that!" said Peter. "It is impossible!"

"But just to make sure," said Arthur.

"We should kill her," they all said together, and then they looked down at me.

In the seconds that followed, there was a strange sound I couldn't place. I thought maybe it was one of the thieves unsheathing their weapon, but then I noticed blood soaking the collar of Peter's shirt, and his head slowly slid off his neck, bouncing as it hit the ground. His body followed, revealing a towering figure with hair as dark as midnight. His brows were lowered over shadowed eyes, his cheeks high but hollowed with anger. He was dressed in fine clothing, finer than the prince of Rook, but I could focus only on the long sword he wielded, dripping with the blood of the thief.

He was fae, and he was beautiful.

For a few seconds, terror rooted me to the spot, but when his gaze shifted to mine, his violent eyes a stunning shade of lilac, I found my footing and scrambled to my feet. As I turned and ran, the two thieves bolted past me, screaming.

Arthur went down at the edge of the forest, a dagger in his back. The other made it into the thick of the wood, and I followed.

I ran so hard, it felt like my bones were splintering. The only thing I could hear was the rustling of flora as the remaining thief and I barreled through the forest to escape the warrior fae.

Beyond the blur of trees, I could make out the thief's retreating form as he stumbled over the ground. His mistake was looking back, though I suspected there was no escaping the fae.

"No! Please!" His voice rang with fear. "No!"

A bloodcurdling scream followed his final words, and then there was silence, save for the sound of my own breathing. I kept running, vaulting over a large branch. I halted and lifted it from the decaying leaves, holding it like a club in my hands as I hid behind an ancient tree, its shallow roots making it hard to stay upright.

It wasn't long before I heard footsteps. I held my breath and waited until they drew near before I stepped out from behind the tree and swung the branch with all my might. It flew through the air and landed a few feet away, not even grazing the head of the fox from last night, who sat patiently before me with his tail curled around his feet.

"What are you doing here?" I asked, relieved to see him and not the fae.

"Your aim was off," said a voice from behind me.

A strangled cry escaped my mouth as I turned and came face-to-face with the fae. I took a step back and fell. Spotting another branch, I tried to reach for it, but it crumbled in my hands, so instead, I squeezed a handful of the decayed limb and threw it at the creature.

I didn't wait to see if I hit him. I got to my feet and ran, but I didn't make it very far before his arm snaked around my waist and he pulled me against his hard body. His hand clamped down on my mouth, silencing the shriek that bubbled from my throat.

"Is that any way to treat your rescuer?" he asked. His breath was warm, and his lips brushed the shell of my ear.

I shivered and closed my eyes, readying myself for the sting of his killing blow, but it didn't come.

"I am a little disappointed you aren't fighting," he said.

I opened my eyes and then jerked away, snatching a limb from the ground. It was a poor weapon in the face of his blade, but it was something. I turned to face him. He looked at the stick and smirked before he met my gaze.

"You had better be careful, Lore," said the fox. "She is a wild one."

"I have no intention of killing you," the fae said.

I narrowed my eyes, suspicious. "Then why did you chase me?"

"I didn't," he said. "I chased your attackers."

"You put your hand over my mouth!"

"You were going to scream."

"Because I thought you were going to kill me!"

"You should not assume," he said.

"You *killed* three other men!" I snapped.

"They were men and thieves," he said. "Are you a man or a thief?"

"Do I look like a man?"

The fae's eyes dipped to my breasts, and he smirked. I swiped at him with my stick. It sounded like a whip as it cut the air toward him, though he caught it easily with one gloved hand and yanked it from my hands.

I recoiled and covered my head with my hands, preparing for his blow.

But nothing came.

Slowly, I straightened, letting my arms fall to my sides. I kept my gaze lowered, unable to face the fae. My cheeks burned with embarrassment.

"What did I tell you, Lore?" said the fox. "This one will break your heart."

I wasn't sure what the fox meant by that, but for some reason, it made me feel worse.

"Look at me, wild one," said the fae.

For some reason, that name only made my face burn hotter. The fae—Lore, according to the fox—took a step toward me, which finally drew my attention to his face. Again, I was struck by his beauty and the strange color of his eyes. I thought that perhaps he was an elf of some kind of status, given the point of his ears and his dress.

"I will never hurt you," he said.

His choice of words were interesting. It implied something beyond this present moment.

"People with kinder eyes have hurt me before," I said.

His gaze remained steady, but his mouth tensed.

"I cannot lie," he answered.

I'd heard that before but never truly believed it, and I didn't now. I considered saying as much, but just as I opened my mouth, I was interrupted by the sound of my name echoing in the Enchanted Forest.

"Samara!"

I whirled in the direction of Michal's voice, but I could not yet see him through the thick brush of the forest.

Panic rose inside me as I looked for a place to hide.

"Do you want to be found?" Lore asked.

My breath seized in my throat as he once again spoke against my ear. He moved so soundlessly, I had not heard him approach. Despite my heart pounding in my chest at the thought of being discovered by my brothers, I hesitated to answer—to trust him. While he had said he had no intention of killing me, there were always worse things.

A shuddering breath escaped my mouth, and I shook my head once.

Suddenly, roots shot from the ground, twisting around us.

Magic, I realized as I craned my neck and turned, watching them close over my head to form the trunk of a tree. My feet slipped on the uneven ground, and I fell against the fae. He caught me, and I tried unsuccessfully to straighten, my hands pressed flat against his chest, but I only managed to step on the fox's tail, and he emitted a horrifying, almost human yelp.

"Sorry," I breathed quietly, still trying to find my footing, but then Lore's hand came around my waist, and he pulled me against him.

I looked up at him, frustrated.

"This is easier," he said.

I glared, though it was hard to keep his gaze, not because his eyes were strange but because he was so beautiful.

This is how mortals die, I thought. *This is how I die.*

He did not seem to have any issue staring at me, his eyes illuminated by a blade of light streaming in from a gap in the twisted trunk.

"Couldn't you have made a larger tree?" I asked.

"Are you going to complain about everything I do?" he asked.

I opened my mouth to apologize, but he put a gloved finger to my lips and hushed me. I let my hands shift down his chest to his sides and held him tighter. This felt safer, though I did not know why.

I watched Lore's face as he turned into the blade of light and eyed my brother's approach.

"Samara!" Michal's voice erupted again, close this time. He was right outside the tree.

I jumped, and Lore held me tighter. I wasn't sure if he intended to comfort me or keep me close so he could silence me if needed.

"Shut up, you imbecile!" Jackal hissed.

At the sound of Jackal's voice, I began to tremble. I curled my fingers into Lore's tunic, trying to force myself into stillness, but it didn't work. Lore continued to hold me, and I made no move to push him away. I thought about how often I'd wanted someone to hold me like this and the irony that it was happening while I was trapped in the trunk of a tree, hiding from my brothers.

The sound of Michal's voice startled me again. I turned my head into a beam of light and realized there was an opening for me to see through too.

I leaned close to peer out. At first, I could only see Michal. Then a pebble flew through the air and hit the back of his head.

"Ouch!" Michal seethed and whirled to face Hans, who snickered as he also walked into view. The two were dressed for a hunt, in their darker clothes and leathers, which I found odd since Prince Henry had left them rich men.

"What?" he snapped. "She can't have gone far."

"Even if she didn't, what makes you think she would come running to us?" asked Hans.

"She will if she is smart," said Michal.

"She didn't leave on her own, idiot!" said Hans.

"How can you tell?"

"You don't really think she killed the prince and the thieves?"

53

"Have you seen her gut a pig?" Michal asked.

Lore gave a quiet laugh that almost sounded like a scoff. I glanced at him. He seemed amused. Maybe he found it hard to imagine I had gutted anything.

"Well, the prince wasn't gutted, and neither were the thieves, were they?" asked Hans. "They were sliced clear in half!"

Hearing that sent a shiver down my spine. Hesitantly, I glanced up at him again. I don't think his gaze ever left me. He didn't speak, but he lifted his hand to my face, brushing my cheek with his thumb. I held my breath. His touch was gentle, as if he were telling me in a different way that he would never hurt me.

I hated that I didn't believe him and turned away from his touch. He dropped his arm from around me, letting me lean closer to the opening.

Outside, my brothers still argued.

"If she didn't kill them, who did?" asked Michal.

"Perhaps she has had a secret lover who helped her escape," said Hans.

"But we have only her footprints and those of a fox," said Michal.

A heavy silence followed, and then suddenly, Michal and Hans looked up, as if they might find me in the trees. Only Jackal remained still and quiet, eyes narrowed and searching, and as I peered between the crack in the tree, his eyes met mine.

Fear ricocheted through me, and I inhaled an audible breath, which I immediately regretted. I covered my mouth with my hands and retreated, tripping over the fox, who let out a sharp yowl. Lore caught my arm before I could fall and dragged me against him. This time, his hold felt like an iron band around my back.

"Did you hear that?" Michal asked.

"It sounded like it was coming from inside that tree," said Hans.

I could see my brothers begin to circle the trunk, and Lore unsheathed a small blade. I wasn't sure what he planned to do with it, as it did not seem like a weapon that could take down any of my brothers but then again, he was fae and they were not. Still, I gripped his forearm, and he looked at me, his eyes searching mine.

"Please," I mouthed, though I did not know why I stopped him. Did I want to protect my brothers, or was I too afraid of being discovered? Truly, I did not know, but I also could not think. The fear was pounding through my veins.

Lore continued to stare, studying my face with a frown.

Then there was a sharp blow to the trunk of the tree. It caused the wood to vibrate around us and the air to fill with dust.

Hans was using his axe to chop the tree.

"Who cares about a fucking fox?" Jackal hissed suddenly. "Who cares how the prince was killed or even the thieves? What matters is that the prince of Rook is dead, and his kingdom will likely offer a great reward to the one who brings his murderer to justice."

"But we do not know who murdered the prince," said Michal.

"No, but our dear, dear sister does, and once we find her, we will surely learn the truth, and we will either present her or her supposed lover to the king as the assailant. Either way, we will be rich."

My brothers were quiet as they processed Jackal's

words. Hans chuckled and then Michal. Their laughter rose, echoing all around me, making my ears ring, but it grew fainter and fainter as they retreated, returning, I guessed, to hide the bodies of the thieves.

"Well, aren't they pleasant," said the fox.

His words broke through my fearful haze, and I released Lore's forearm. My fingers ached from holding him so tight. I ignored the embarrassment I felt at having done so and peered out the hole in the tree, suspicious that my brothers were still near, waiting to pounce.

But then the tree disappeared, and I yelped as I fell to my hands and knees. I hurried to my feet and turned to face Lore as he sheathed the knife he'd drawn earlier.

He continued to look unhappy, and I wondered what I had done wrong.

"Your brothers are idiots," said Lore.

"They are heroes," I said. "Without them, my village would starve."

His eyes flitted down my body. I didn't like the way he looked at me, like he was frustrated with what he saw.

"What about you?" he asked.

"What about me?"

"What happens to you without them?"

My mouth parted, my answer poised on the tip of my tongue.

Then I am free, I wanted to say, but that was just a dream, and dreams were only achieved by wishing, and no one wished in this land—not without consequences.

"I suppose I would die," I said.

Lore stared at me, his eyes like violet fire.

"Within seven days?" he asked.

"What?" I asked, confused by his question.

"If you are without them for seven days, will you die?"

"Well, no," I said. "Of course not."

"And you said her brothers were idiots," said the fox.

I looked at him, narrowing my gaze.

"What's going on? First you come to me at the moor and warn me that my carriage will be attacked, and now you are here with the fae who saved me. Was this planned?"

I felt silly saying it aloud. Why would either of them make a plan to save me?

Lore and the fox exchanged a glance before returning their attention to me.

"Your brothers hired the thieves to attack your carriage. I believe their intentions were to kill the thieves and pose as the hero to the king of Rook but...Prince Lore got to you first."

My gaze snapped to the fae's.

"Prince?"

Lore raised a dark brow. "Yes?"

"You did not say you were a prince," I said.

I had tried to hit him and thrown wood in his face.

"We hardly had time for formal introductions," he replied. "Besides, I am not the first prince to make your acquaintance."

"Do not let him fool you, wild one," said the fox. "He was quite miffed over that."

Miffed?

Over me?

I had to be dreaming.

I closed my eyes and opened them again, but the fox and the fae still remained, watching.

"Perhaps I am dead," I said.

"You are very much alive," said Lore. "At least you

have promised to be for the next seven days, which will bode well for me, since I am in need of a mortal, and you are now in my debt."

I swallowed hard, looking at him.

"Excuse me?"

"I saved your life," he said, as if that explained everything.

I stared at him and then asked, "Did I ask you to?"

He blinked. "What?"

"You say I owe you a debt because you saved my life, but I did not ask you to save my life."

Lore tilted his head as if he did not understand me. "Are you saying you did not want to be saved?"

"I don't know," I said. I could not remember what I had been thinking before he killed Peter. "The point is that I did not ask, and how can there be a debt if I did not ask?"

The fox made a strange, high-pitched sound, a laugh, I realized. "Oh, she is a clever thing," he said. "If I did not know better, I'd think she were fae!"

Lore scowled and took a step toward me. I curled my fingers into fists.

"It does not matter that you didn't ask," he said. "You are obligated to repay me however I choose, and I *have* chosen."

I did not understand.

"Why me?" I asked.

"Why *not* you?" he asked.

"I am…worthless," I said.

I had no skills, save keeping house, and still, as my brothers often reminded me, I managed to fail at that every day.

Lore studied me for a few quiet seconds, and in that time, I felt like the only thing in existence. He lifted his hand

58

but did not touch me, only let his fingers mimic brushing my skin. I could feel their heat, even gloved. It was enough.

"You do not get to determine your worth to me," he said and dropped his hand.

I stared at him, considering my options, though there truly was only one—to follow him and fulfill my debt. It was not as if I could go home.

"My brothers will come for me," I said. "They have hunted and survived this forest many times."

"So have I," he replied. "I will keep you safe."

A thrill went through me, warm and pleasurable. I longed to contain it, because I did not want to feel it. Fae would say anything to get their way, and I doubted this one was any different. He had, after all, saved me for a purpose that only served him. I would have to remember that if I was going to survive this.

"And after seven days?" I asked. "What happens to me if I have not managed to repay you?"

"Nothing," he said. "You will be free."

I almost laughed at his words but stopped myself. He did not understand—he did not know. I might be free of him, but I would never be free of my brothers.

Lore frowned and then asked, "Do you desire something else?"

I held his gaze as I answered in a hushed tone. "I have never desired anything else."

"Truly?" he asked, his voice just as quiet, and I refused to think about the fae I had loved and all I had dreamed for us.

"Truly," I said, glad that at least I could lie.

CHAPTER FOUR
The Cursed Prince

LORE

Foul humans with their foul mouths.

My hatred for Samara's brothers grew the longer I remained within the presence of this woman who flinched when I lifted a finger and looked at me as if I were the one who had harmed her.

It was a bitter irony given she was the one who had rejected *my* kindness, severing *my* hand with the very knife I had given her, a blade so sharp it could hew a stone in two.

That was seven years ago, and still I felt the pain of that day. It went beyond the phantom ache in my limb. This woman had carved her name in my heart long ago, and I still bled from that open wound.

She was my curse, and I wanted to be free.

"What did you choose?" Samara asked.

I blinked, so lost in my own thoughts, I had trouble tracking hers.

"What?"

"You said you had chosen how I will repay you," she said. "What did you choose?"

I watched her mouth as she spoke. There was something beautiful about the way words formed on her lips. It was not a helpful observation for my cock, which was growing inconveniently harder the longer I looked at her.

"Your Highness?"

I wanted her to say my name. I wanted to hear it in the dead of night while she lay beneath me, overcome with pleasure.

I ground my teeth, frustrated by my thoughts but it was also a reminder of why I'd rescued this woman and brought her into my world.

"I need you to break my curse," I said.

Before she could respond, I turned toward the fox.

"Lead the way, Fox. We only have seven days."

"As you command, Prince," said the fox, who rose and trotted off into the forest.

The trees were thick, their limbs heavy with thorned garland and wild grape vines. The ground was covered with an intricate tangle of tree roots, ferns, and wood anemone that bloomed white, stark against the sea of green. There were other flowers too, but they were not so dense—purple violets, pale pink gooseberry, and a colony of red bleeding heart. Their magic called to me like music, their petals like pretty bells chiming in the wind. Their scent was just as powerful. Some of it was honeyed and healing, and some of it was metallic and toxic, but nothing could overpower Samara, who smelled like sweet oleander. As enticing as it was, I was the Prince of Nightshade, and I knew that the sweetest things were sometimes the most poisonous.

With Samara, it had only taken a glance—a glimpse of her pale face, rosy lips, and coal-black hair—and it was done. That was how I knew I was cursed, because there was no such thing as love at first sight, yet here I was, completely ensnared and unable to escape her as she stumbled around behind me in an attempt to navigate the tangled wood.

Everything about her was *loud*. Her footsteps were like water crashing upon rocks, her breathing like the howling wind, and she was as slow as a snail. If this was to be our pace, I would fail to break my curse in seven days. I considered carrying her, but the thought of touching her made my body feel too warm and too tight. It was exciting to the point that it repulsed me.

"My lord?" Samara spoke softly but breathlessly.

I recognized her hesitancy as fear, and I did not like it, but I knew her brothers were responsible. They had been terrible since the moment I met her seven years ago. I would have killed them had she not stopped me. I did not understand why she protected them. I had killed my own brothers a time or two for far lesser offenses, though the action was futile. They just came back, worse than before.

I didn't look at her or ease my stride.

"You may call me Lore," I said, my voice tight. I wondered if it was a mistake to let her say my name, yet pressure built in my chest as I waited for her to speak it.

She didn't.

"May I ask you a question?" she asked.

I took a breath and let it out slowly, attempting to dispel the disappointment.

"You may," I said. As much as I dreaded what she might ask, I did not want to tell her no.

"Why are you cursed?"

"I looked at an enchantress, and now I cannot escape her," I said. It was close enough to the truth.

"It seems rather extreme to curse someone for staring," she said.

Ahead of us, the fox snorted. "His Highness has cursed many for far less."

I glared at the creature, thinking that I'd like to show him what it was to be cursed and sentence him to wear his fur inside out for the rest of his life, but I resisted the urge for vengeance. Samara was so used to horror, I did not want to become another monster in her eyes.

"Perhaps that is why you are cursed," said Samara.

Her comment frustrated me, and I paused, turning to face her.

"Are you implying that I deserve to be cursed?"

She ceased to breathe as I watched her, growing pale. I did not even know why it mattered what she thought; she was mortal and had no understanding of the world that flourished beneath the boughs of the Enchanted Forest. Still, I desired to know.

"No, my lord," she said.

"Then what are you saying?" I wanted to close the distance between us, but I did not want to watch her cower before me.

"Ignore me, my lord. I know not what I speak."

"Do you dislike my name?" I asked, tilting my head to the side as I watched her.

For a second, she looked confused. "No, my lord."

"Then why don't you use it?"

She opened her mouth to speak, but then she closed it and lowered her head. "I apologize...*Lore*."

"I do not want an apology," I said. "I want to know what you really think."

She watched me like prey shivering beneath the eyes of a wolf.

"I won't hurt you. I have promised, and I cannot break a promise," I said.

"It does not matter that you cannot break promises. I do not trust you," she said. "I will call you Lore when I trust you."

My chest felt tight, like she had taken a hold of my heart. I did not want to feel disappointed by her words. Lore was not even my true name, but that was not a name I would offer for the same reason, as eager as I was to hear her say it. It was a reckless thought. The gift of a true name was the offer of power. I could not deny her anything if she spoke it, though I knew I'd deny her nothing no matter what she chose to call me.

That was the danger of this curse.

I dipped my chin and held her gaze. "As you desire," I said. "And?"

"And what, my lord?" She used my title deliberately, as if to emphasize her point, her eyes alight with challenge. I wasn't even sure she realized it, and if I pointed it out, she'd likely crawl back into her shell, so I said nothing, only smirked, liking this peek at who she could have been—maybe who she still *could* be—without her brothers.

"You have an opinion on why I am cursed," I said. "I want to know it."

She took a breath, lifting her chin. She did not

answer my question but asked one instead "Why do you curse people?"

I had not thought much about it. I suppose people just annoyed me, but I did not want to say that aloud.

"To teach lessons," I said.

It wasn't untrue, even if the lesson was leaving me alone.

"What kind of lessons?" she asked.

I hesitated. *Oh, she was challenging.*

"I suppose that depends on the offense," I said.

She watched me, and I waited, anxious for her approval.

"I do not think anyone deserves to be cursed," she said. "But if the purpose of a curse is to learn a lesson, what is yours?"

"I was not cursed to learn a lesson," I said.

There was no point in loving someone who did not love you back. Whoever had brought this upon me—likely one of my beastly brothers—intended one thing—*torture*.

I turned and began walking again.

"But isn't that how curses are broken?" she asked as she followed.

"Not this one," I said.

"Then I do not understand how I am supposed to break this curse."

"You aren't going to break it," I said. "You will wish it away."

It took me a moment, but I soon realized that Samara had stopped following. I paused and turned, but she was gone. Instantly, dread pooled in the pit of my stomach.

"Samara!" I jogged back to the place where I'd seen

her last and looked in all directions but saw only dense, green foliage. It was as though she'd vanished. "Fuck!"

"You dimwit," said the fox. "You scared her!"

"I did not intend to!" I said. "She didn't even give me a chance to explain!"

"She told you she did not trust you," said the fox. "Yet you led with a wish!"

"I am aware," I snapped. I had a feeling she would remind me often, with her actions and her words, but if she'd given me a chance, I'd have told her about the wishing tree and its magic. "Fuck," I muttered again, scanning the ground for signs of her footsteps when I noticed a sprawling shrub with leafy, dark green vines. Purple flowers grew in clusters along their stems, and some had turned into bright red berries. It was bitter nightshade, and like all plants of its kind, they were singing.

There once lived a prince of poison
Who marked a mortal as his chosen.
But she did not want to be his wife
So she severed his hand with a knife,
And now his heart is broken.

I ground my teeth. Despite my power, I often battled the singsong nightshades. The forest had influence first, and she took great joy in taunting me, which had given me a specific reputation among the fae, since no one heard what I heard.

"I will poison you to the root if you do not tell me where she has gone," I growled.

The nightshade shivered, and their tune changed quickly.

Look close, Prince.
See our limbs, they are limp.
See our leaves, they are ripped.
Your lover, she came this way.
Your lover, she ran this way!

The bitter nightshade continued to repeat the verse as I followed the broken path Samara had left trampling through the forest to escape me.

Escape. That word twisted through me. As much as I wanted to be rid of this curse, this obsession, I wanted to be the one Samara never feared.

"Are you ever going to tell her?" the fox asked. He lingered behind me, trotting along as if nothing were wrong.

"Tell her what, Fox?" I asked, frustrated.

"Who you are," he said. "That you are the hand who offered the knife."

"Why would I tell her such a thing? She showed how she felt seven years ago," I said, not wanting to face her rejection again.

"Perhaps you are wrong."

"How can I be wrong when my hand is gone?" I asked.

"Her brothers, they are terrible things," said the fox. "Have you considered that they may be why you lost your hand?"

"Of course I have considered," I said. "But nothing changes that she held the knife."

"Surely, that is not true."

Honestly, I did not know, but it was easier to believe. She had already rejected me once, and I did not want to face it again.

"What I need most right now is to keep Samara from running so she can break my curse," I said. After that, I would be free, and so would she, and neither of us would ever think of the other again.

"Are you sure you are cursed?" asked the fox.

"Of course I am sure. She is all I ever think about!"

For the last seven years, she was all I ever dreamed about.

"Have you tried thinking of something else?"

"Of course I have!" I roared, annoyed by the fox's ridiculous words. I had tried to think of *anything* else. I'd gone to the very edge of the world and sat with the sun, moon, and stars and still thought of nothing but her. She was unmatched—brighter than the sun, more beautiful than the moon, sweeter than the stars. I loved her more than anything in this terrible world, and I hated it. "I cannot escape her."

"Apparently, you can," said the fox. "Or at the very least, she can escape *you*."

I growled low in my throat. "I hate you, Fox."

"Mutual, Prince," he said.

As we continued, a persistent thump echoed throughout the wood. At first, it was faint, but the farther we walked, the louder it grew, and so did my dread. It was soon joined by the sound of flutes and fiddles. It was the sound of fae revelry, and it had likely drawn Samara's attention, as it would many unlucky mortals tonight.

Just ahead, there came an old fae woman who was no bigger than a crow, her wings beating hard and fast. She wore a skirt of green grass and a shirt made from the petals of a poppy. She carried an umbrella made from maple leaves to keep the sun off her skin, which was so pale, it was almost translucent. Without it, she would surely burn to death.

"Fair maiden," I said.

"I cannot delay, my lord," she said, her voice high-pitched like a small bell. "For I must be off to the marsh where the night raven sleeps."

I followed beside her. "I will join you on your journey if you tell me from where that music comes."

"It comes from the elfin hill," she said. "The maidens are practicing their dances."

There were many elfin hills of varying sizes. Some were small and some were large, some housed tiny fae and some housed larger fae, and unless they were open, they merely appeared to be grassy mounds.

"For whom are they practicing?" I asked.

"Why, for the old elf king's honorable guests," she said.

"Would I know them, fair maiden?"

"I am certain I would not know," she said. "For I do not know you."

I gritted my teeth but tried not to show my frustration.

"If the maidens are practicing their dances and the old elf king has invited many distinguished guests, then there must be much to celebrate," I said.

"Oh, there will be, but only if every maiden ends the night betrothed," said the fae.

"Are there many eligible maidens?" I asked.

"Oh yes, for the music you have heard will only reach the ears of those who are unwed, even mortals."

I no longer had any doubt as to where Samara had gone.

"Tell me, fair maiden, who is invited tonight?"

"Anyone may come to the ball, which will take place after the banquet, but the banquet is only for the elf king's honorable guests," she said. "Now, I have delayed too long, and there is much still to do. I must be on my way as I have yet to send the invitations, and the night raven will wake soon."

"Fair maiden, you have been so busy. Allow me to assist you," I said. "If you tell me who is invited, I will go to the night raven for you."

"What a dear," she said. "If you will do me this favor, then you may come to the ball this night!"

"I am at your service," I said, bowing very slightly.

The old elf maid smiled so wildly and with much relief and then began speaking. "His first visit must be to Nereus and his daughters, who will likely not stay long, for they do not want to be gone from the sea. Still, we shall try to make them comfortable. We must ask the brownies, though it is nighttime, and they may not want to abandon their chores. Oh, and do not forget the trolls—not the giant ones, for they will stomp on the ground and cause much strife, but the ones with tails who are smaller and can fit beneath the hilltop."

The longer the fae rattled on, the more I regretted my decision, but I thought about Samara dancing beneath the moonlight for men who were not me, which reminded me why I needed to do this.

"I am hesitant to ask the ghosts, but I fear they will haunt our guests if I do not. But if we invite the ghosts, we must also invite the *gloson* and keep him well fed, or he will seek food among our guests."

"Of course, fair maiden," I said quickly, interrupting her before she could add more creatures to her list of guests. "Is there anything else you may need? You so smartly mentioned food. Perhaps there is something I could fetch for the old king's distinguished guests."

"What a blessing you are!" she said. "I daresay, our guests of honor—the goblin king and his sons—would enjoy a few rusty nails, but they must be from the foot of a bone horse, for those are a delicacy. If you return with them before sundown, you may have a seat at the banquet."

"Does the goblin king seek a wife?"

"For his two sons," she said. "Though they are rumored to be careless and rude."

"Pity the women they choose," I said.

"Nay, good sir," she said. "For the maidens shall become princesses, and their husbands will inherit many castles and goblin gold."

"I'd rather the castles and gold," I said.

"Well, perhaps the goblin king's sons will like the look of you, and then you will have castles and gold. Now off with you!" she said and called out as she turned. "The night raven will wake soon!"

There was silence for a few seconds, and then the fox spoke.

"Surely, a prince of your rank would be an honored guest? Wouldn't it have been easier to tell the old elf maid who you were?"

"No," I said. I was lucky she had not recognized me, and I hoped the same would be true tonight at the ball. Otherwise, I would fail to rescue Samara. "Trust me, it will be far easier to pry nails from the feet of a bone horse."

CHAPTER FIVE
The Elfin Hill

SAMARA

You will wish it away.

As soon as those words left the Prince of Nightshade's lips, I ran. I had made one wish in my life, and it had only led to horror. I swore I would never make another, and I certainly wouldn't for someone else, no matter the debt I owed.

He would just have to hunt me.

Though he may not get the chance if my brothers found me first, which was more likely now that I had fled from the prince's side. Despite the threat, I was willing to give the forest a chance. I doubted it was any more threatening than the men in my life.

I kept running, weaving what I hoped was a confusing path through the forest. I tore buttons from my cloak and pieces from my dress, leaving them scattered along a path I quickly abandoned for a new direction. Once I felt safe enough, I would stop and devise a plan.

I had few options. I could not go home or anywhere near Gnat. There were other towns within the shadow of the Enchanted Forest I might be able to reach, but then there was still the matter of the debt I owed to the prince and the lengths the forest would go to see that I fulfill it. Even with all this, I'd rather try something— *anything*. Even if I died in the process, at least it would be under my control.

As I ran, I glanced over my shoulder to see if anyone was following, when suddenly, my foot dropped into a hole and I fell, striking my knees on moss-covered rocks. Everything hurt, even my hands, which I had used to catch myself. Maybe I wouldn't have to worry about anyone finding me. Maybe the forest would swallow me whole.

I pulled my foot out from between the rocks. It hurt and was already swollen. I sat for a moment to catch my breath, my chest and ribs aching as I scanned my surroundings, realizing that what I'd thought was just a grassy hill was actually a slope covered in large boulders. Trees sprouted from between them, their branches like bony hands clawing at the air. They'd stopped growing long ago and now seemed to be frozen in time, covered in vibrant, green moss from which golden poppies grew.

It was beautiful, but the descent would be treacherous. I would have to change directions again, but as I got to my feet, there was a faint breeze. I had grown so hot from running, the sudden brush of cool air sent needlelike chills down my spine. Or perhaps it was not the wind so much as the music it carried. It was airy and soft, and I could barely hear it, but I couldn't let it go.

It was beckoning, and I wanted to follow it, which meant a descent through the labyrinth of boulders at my feet. The first step was the hardest and most painful. The second wasn't so bad, and by the third, I could manage the pain if I gritted my teeth hard enough.

There was no true path down, only a narrow space of rocky earth that was sometimes overgrown with moss or ferns. Farther downhill, the boulders towered, and while the path was smoother, it was overgrown with flora. I had no choice but to wade through vibrant poppies as they danced in clusters around my feet. I thought they might be swaying to the music, which was closer now and more distinct. A drum had joined the ensemble, and I took a step with each beat. Soon, the pain in my ankle receded, but my eyes had grown heavy, and I suddenly had the overwhelming urge to sleep.

I stumbled and fell, finding that the earth beneath me was cushioned, far softer than anything I'd ever slept on in my twenty-six years. I tried to rise, but my body was too heavy, and my arms shook with the effort.

"Sleep," I heard the flowers say, their voices like a soft hum, a lullaby cradling my body. "We will keep you safe."

I opened my eyes, and I swore the poppies grew taller, blocking out the sun and sky and the twisted branches of the ancient oaks above me until there was nothing but darkness, and I fell asleep believing them more than I believed Lore.

———

Something poked me.

I woke instantly, heart already racing as I pushed myself up and scrambled away, expecting to see my brothers standing over me, but as my vision cleared, I realized it was not my brothers who had touched me but a fairy.

She was small, no taller than the poppy stem she gripped between her small hands. She looked as though she were made from a tree, with skin like bark and hair like braided vines. A dryad, I realized. She wore a dress made of dark leaves and rosettes, and the entire thing seemed to shimmer like dew in the early morning light, except it was not early morning at all. It was dusk, and the sky had turned orange in color.

"Oh," I said, rubbing my eyes. "I am so sorry. I thought…you were someone else."

She stared at me with her large, mossy eyes and asked, "Are you going to the ball?"

I blinked, confused. "The ball?"

"There is a ball down at the old elfin hill," she said. "If you do not hurry, you will miss the dancing!"

"That sounds lovely," I said. "But I am afraid I was not invited."

"You do not have to be invited, silly!" she said. "Everyone may come! The old elf king has declared it so!"

I hesitated again. "I would disgrace him," I said, looking down at my tattered and worn dress. It was the only thing I'd worn the last ten years. I had mended it to the point that it was now mostly thread and not cloth at all. "I have only these rags to wear."

"Then we shall dress you," said the dryad.

"Please," I said. "I would not ask that of you."

I did not feel comfortable with the thought of

accepting such a gift, especially from the fae. Lore had already taught me that nothing was done out of kindness. Everything was an exchange, and I wondered what a pretty new dress would cost.

"You didn't," she said. "I have offered. All I ask is that you come to the ball."

I considered the dryad's offer, half-afraid this was a trap.

"What does one do at a fae ball?" I asked.

"What an odd question!" she said. "Why, dance and sing and eat until dawn!"

At the mention of food, my stomach rumbled. I could not remember when I had eaten last. Plus, I had never been to a ball before, and it sounded far more fun than wandering through the Enchanted Forest in the dark.

"And...will I be able to leave?" I asked.

"Mortals are so contrary," said the dryad, her brows furrowing. "Of course you can leave."

If that was the case, then I saw no harm in attending.

"Then I will come to the ball with you," I said.

The dryad smiled, pleased, and then leapt into the air, her wings glittering as they trilled behind her. "Hurry then! You must follow me!"

I rose from the flowers with no pain in my ankle and paused to inspect it. There was no sign I had injured it, no swelling or bruising.

"What's the matter?" asked the dryad, hovering near. "We must be on our way!"

"I am only amazed," I said. "Before I fell asleep in the flowers, I had injured my foot."

"The poppies must have healed you," she said. "For that is what they do, either heal or kill."

She zipped away then, somersaulting through the air,

and I followed, again falling into step with the music, which I now felt vibrating in my veins. Before long, we emerged from behind the final row of boulders where the forest was open and endless. When we stepped beneath those ancient and heavy limbs, hundreds of lights ignited within the trees.

"Oh," I said, breathless, awed by the beautiful display.

As I looked closer, I saw that there were hundreds of fairies in the branches, holding lanterns.

"We will carry the lanterns to the elfin hill," said the dryad. "Come, or we will be late!"

I followed her past many trees until we came to the largest one. It was bigger than any tree I had ever seen. Perhaps it was the oldest within the Enchanted Forest, though I doubted anyone could say for certain. Its branches were dense and heavy with many needles and red berries.

"Old Mother!" called the dryad, knocking on the trunk. "Old Mother! I have a mortal here in need of some clothes!"

It took me a moment to realize that the tree was moving. Suddenly, an arm broke free from the trunk and then a leg, and before long, an entire creature made of wood stood before me. She was about my height and had deep eyes, a wide nose, and a frowning mouth. Moss and mushrooms grew on her head and arms, trailing down her trunk.

"A mortal, you say?" asked Old Mother. She leaned in to look at me, creaking like long limbs in the wind, her empty eyes unblinking. "What a pretty, pale thing. Are you sure she is not a ghost?"

"I am not a ghost, Old Mother," I said, though my voice was quiet.

"No?" asked the old dryad. She lifted her limb-like hand to my chin, and I stiffened at her touch. "Your eyes say otherwise. Your eyes say you want to disappear."

I'm not sure why I blushed. Perhaps it was because she had seen to my soul. I did not know what to say, so I did not speak. Instead, I dropped my gaze.

"It is all right, pretty thing," she said. "Tonight, you will know what it is to be admired."

I started to protest. I did not need to be admired, but Old Mother stopped me.

"Ah, ah, ah," she said. "I will not hear it. You shall be the belle of the ball."

She reached behind her head, broke something off with a quick snap, and offered a walnut.

"Open," she instructed.

I looked at Old Mother and then at the nut. I did not want to insult her, so I took it, feeling strange as I bit into the woody shell and then pried it apart to reveal a bundle of white fabric. I pulled it out, dropping the shell, and found that it was a beautiful gown.

"Oh, Old Mother," I said, holding the dress to my chest. "I have never had anything so beautiful!"

"Put it on! Put it on!"

My eyes widened, and I glanced around.

"Behind my tree, pretty thing!" she said.

I hurried around the yew and found an opening in the bark that was just big enough for me to fit. A strange excitement went through me as I undressed. I had not had anything new in such a long time, much less something so beautiful.

As I slipped into the new dress, I was surprised by its softness and how perfectly it fit. The skirt was frilled but light and airy, like gossamer floating in the wind. Lace threaded with silver and garlands of pretty white roses dangled from the waist at different lengths. The bodice was corseted and cut like the top of a heart, embellished with the same lace and roses. The sleeves were nothing more than long ribbons of gauze fabric tied on my shoulders.

"Pretty thing, are you ready?" called the younger dryad.

"I…I cannot lace the back," I said.

"Come, pretty thing, and I will do it for you."

I stepped out from the cover of the tree to find the dryad hovering, wings beating fast.

"Turn around, pretty thing," she said and then pulled the laces of the corset tight. When she was finished, I turned to her, burying my hands in the skirt of my new dress. I did not think I'd be able to stop touching it.

"Oh, you are a vision," said the dryad. "Old Mother is never wrong! You shall be the belle of the ball!"

I smiled because I could not help it. I was going to a ball!

"Off with you now!" Old Mother said as we rounded her tree. "Off to the ball, pretty thing!"

The dryads descended from the canopy above, their lanterns flickering as they flew. I smiled at Old Mother and then followed the light. It was like running beneath the stars. As the dryads lit the way, they seemed to draw all manner of creatures from the dark—fairies with butterfly wings and brownies in strange hats, dwarves dressed in fine jewels. There were also nymphs, small ones and tall ones, some with wings and some without, some with white hair and some with brown.

One danced up to me, her arm laden with floral crowns, and placed one upon my head before twirling away. Another came up to me and took my hand in hers, giggling and smiling as she pulled me along. We skipped to the music, which was closer now than before, a soft but warm and rich sound that was deeper than bells but higher than drums. The melody was hypnotic, and my body was buzzing.

I had never been so happy, and I did not know what spurred it, the feeling of being included and seen or some other kind of magic.

The dryads parted in the air, forming two lines that looped and then tangled in the trees as we spilled into a meadow, already packed with all kinds of creatures and mortals alike. There were even more fairies and nymphs, some so small they flitted through the air like gnats, others taller than me. There were goblins with long teeth and sharp nails and trolls with tails, centaurs with hooved feet and long beards and fauns with short legs and horns. I had never seen so many creatures before, and there were even more I did not recognize, but they were all soon forgotten as I was pulled into a dance by the nymph who had taken my hand.

As we formed a circle, I looked at her, her eyes so bright, they were like glowing stars.

"I have never danced," I said.

"It is easy. Follow my lead!" she said and pulled me to left and right, skipping as she went. Our circle tightened, and the nymphs beside me raised my arms high, releasing them to clap and spin before we joined hands to do it all over again. By the third turn, I was moving with an ease I'd never felt before and smiling so wide my face hurt. I felt like I could dance forever, even as I grew breathless and hot beneath the dryads' glimmering lights.

The music continued, transforming into something far faster. The nymphs kept hold of my hands, our circle shrinking as a larger one formed around us. I was unprepared as I was jerked to the right, the fae beside me skipping quickly, and then suddenly, they released my hand to take a step and turn. I followed their lead and joined hands with a man, or I thought he was a man, except that his eyes were yellow and his irises black slits.

I held his gaze for a moment, unnerved by those strange eyes set within such a handsome face, until I found myself in the larger circle and pulled again to the right.

We continued like that, coming together and then apart, and I thought that I had never been happier, but as I moved to take another's hand, I realized the dancers were being watched, though that might not have bothered me if it wasn't for one set of eyes.

Lore.

Now that I was aware of him, I didn't know how I'd gone this long without feeling his gaze upon me. It was heavy and dark and...*angry*.

He sat stiffly at the end of a long banquet table, which was positioned beneath a hill that looked as if it had been propped up with grand posts, wound with green garlands. One of his hands rested on the table, gloved fingers tapping but not to the music. He was dressed differently, not in his leather and armor but in a silver tunic with sterling clasps. He was crowned with pale white branches, and his long, silky hair fell over his shoulders.

He was stunning but also terrifying, and the sight of him halted my steps, and then suddenly, no one was dancing, and everyone was staring at me and the Prince of Nightshade.

"My lady?" a voice asked.

It took me a moment to disengage from Lore's stare, a moment to prepare myself for what it would feel like to have his gaze burning up my body. Finally, I turned my head and met the pale yellow eyes of the man I'd first traded places with during the dance.

"Perhaps you would like to rest?" he asked. "Allow me to escort you."

He offered his hand, and I took it, not knowing what else to do. I did not think I could continue dancing now that I knew Lore was here and watching.

The stranger led me from the center of the meadow to a stack of stones that acted as a table and chairs. When I was seated, the music began again.

"Here you are, my lady," he said, handing me a large leaf with which I could fan myself, though I did not think it would help. My body wasn't hot from dancing anymore. This heat burned low and hot in the pit of my stomach.

"Thank you," I said, but the man did not seem to hear me, because he was waving over a servant carrying a tray upon which were a number of silver goblets. He took two and handed me one. I did not know what was in the cup, but I sipped it anyway and found that it was sweet.

The man did too and sat opposite me at the small round table.

"You are human," he said.

I hesitated. "Yes," I said. "Is it so obvious?"

"Only because you cannot dance," he said with a chuckle.

I blushed and took another sip of the sweet drink.

"Do not be embarrassed," he said. "I find it endearing."

I had never been called that before, and I found myself wondering if that was a good thing. It almost felt like being called naive, which I didn't like, though I knew it was true, especially when it came to survival in the Enchanted Forest.

"And you? Are you...human?" I asked, knowing he was not.

He held my gaze and smiled faintly before looking toward the dancers.

"My mother was human," he said. "My father was a goblin."

That explained his eyes.

"Are they still with you?" I asked.

"They died a very long time ago," he said.

It took me a moment to respond. I considered only saying I was sorry, but apologies were strange when the topic was death.

"Mine too," I said.

"Then we both know grief," he said.

I nodded, and we were quiet for a few moments.

"Tell me something about them," I said. "Your mother and father."

I couldn't place the look on the half goblin's face.

"Only if you want to, of course," I added, feeling silly.

"I want to," he said. Then he took a breath and looked away again. "My mother used to sing to me. She had a beautiful voice. Sometimes I think I can still hear her, but only when it is very quiet and the world is still."

"That is not often," I said.

He laughed. "No, not often at all."

"My mother liked to sing too," I said, and I could not help smiling as I remembered the sound. "She was terrible, but she loved it."

The half goblin laughed.

"Do you sing?" he asked.

My smile faded at his question. I did not expect it to be painful, to remind me that I had not sung since my mother died and that I had not felt happy enough to even try.

"I haven't in a long time," I said.

"You sound so lovely when you speak, I am certain you must when you sing."

"I am certain you are wrong, my lord," I said, growing uneasy beneath his praise. I looked away, regretting it instantly when I found Lore staring. He had not moved, and he still seemed angry.

The half goblin must have noticed how I stiffened and followed my gaze. He turned back to me, our eyes meeting.

"Do you know the Prince of Nightshade?" he asked.

"We are acquainted," I said, not wanting to disclose that I was in the prince's debt. "But I would not say I know him."

The half goblin studied me. I did not think he believed me.

"I am surprised he is here. He is not usually welcomed by the fae outside his kingdom."

My chest tightened. "Why?"

"They say he talks to himself and hears things no one else can."

"Is that all?" I asked, frowning. "It seems cruel to exclude him for something so...harmless."

"Is the way he looks at you harmless?"

I didn't know, though he had promised not to hurt me, so maybe it was.

"He is angry with me," I said.

"That is not anger," replied the half goblin.

Before I could ask what it was, a dwarf approached to whisper in his ear. The exchange was brief, but then he turned to me.

"I apologize," he said, rising. "I have been summoned away."

"Of course. Thank you for keeping me company."

"May I?" he asked, holding out his hand.

I hesitated for only a moment but accepted, his fingers clasping mine. He bent and brushed his lips across my skin.

"It was a pleasure," he said. There was an intensity to his gaze that made me blush, and I watched him as he retreated toward the banquet table, though it was not long before my gaze drifted to Lore again. This time, however, he was gone. My heart began to beat fast and my ears started to ring, but before I could scan the crowd for him, a voice interrupted my alarm.

"I hope you did not give him your name, wild one," said a familiar voice, though it startled me. I looked down to find Fox sitting stoically at my feet.

"He did not ask," I said. "But why should I not?"

"Names have power," said the fox. "You do not want to give away your power."

I frowned. Another thing that required an exchange.

"Why are you here, Fox?" I asked.

"I should ask you the same thing, wild one," he said.

"The dryads invited me," I said. "They said all were welcome."

The fox's eyes narrowed, and he tilted his head. "Did they tell you anything else, wild one?"

Dread crept into my chest at his question.

"That I could leave," I said.

"One thing you must learn about fae is that just because they cannot lie does not mean they tell the truth."

"I do not understand—"

"Perhaps you may leave," said the fox. "But only if you are engaged before sunrise."

"What?" I asked breathlessly, shock striking my heart.

"You are dressed as a maiden seeking a husband, clad in white and crowned. Someone here must ask for your hand. Otherwise, you will spend a year inside the elfin hill."

"That cannot be," I said.

"It is," said the fox, his gaze moving past me. "Though you may have no trouble leaving. It seems the goblin king has taken a liking to you."

"Goblin king?" I asked, peering over my shoulder to find the half goblin from earlier standing at the banquet table beside a very small elven man who was so wrinkled, he looked as though he'd melted on the stack of pillows beneath him. They were watching me.

I turned back to the fox. "You must help me," I said. "I do not want—"

My words died on my lips as someone approached, and I looked up to meet Lore's violet eyes.

"Wild one," he said.

I swallowed hard. Up close, he did not look so angry, but his eyes were still bright, burning like an ethereal fire.

"Prince," I said and slowly rose to my feet.

He offered his hand. "Dance with me."

I hesitated, uncertain, given what he wanted from me.

"Samara?" he said. The name was low, barely a whisper. It felt strangely like a spell, and I thought about what the fox had said, about names having power.

I gave Lore my hand, and he led me to the edge of the meadow. We stood apart and the distance felt strange.

"I do not know how to dance," I said.

"You seemed to know earlier," he replied. "Though if you find you are lost, look for me."

The music began, and he bowed his head. I looked about, finding that the ladies curtsied, so I did the same. We rose and circled each other, only to repeat the same move, our eyes never leaving the other.

"You ran," he said.

"I will not wish for you," I said.

I noticed his mouth tighten, but then we turned away from each other, moving in a wide loop until we came face-to-face again. He held out his hand, and I took it as we stepped together and apart.

"I am not asking you to speak it into the ether," he said.

"Then what are you asking?"

We paused as we made another loop around each other, but this time, Lore took another fae's hand while I dipped beneath their arms. I looked at the other dancers, feeling ridiculous as I danced this strange dance, but I remembered Lore's words and turned to him.

He took my hand again.

"I am asking you to accompany me on a quest to find the wishing tree upon which golden apples grow," he said. "When we find it, you must pick one and only take a bite to wish me free. It is that simple."

It sounded too wonderful to be true, which had been the case for everything in my life so far. The fae who had offered the knife, the prince who had offered for my hand.

"You cannot think I believe such a thing exists," I said.

"I cannot lie."

"Perhaps you cannot lie, but you do not have to tell the truth."

Lore's eyes narrowed. "Did the fox tell you that?"

I did not answer, but it was easy to avoid as we turned away from each other.

"I am telling you truthfully, the wishing tree exists," he said when we met again. "But its magic only works on the first night of the full moon."

I did not want to believe him, but he spoke with such sincerity, not only about the tree but also his curse. He seemed desperate to be free.

"That does not explain why I must make the wish."

"You must make the wish because I am unworthy," he said.

I stumbled, and Lore caught me. I righted myself, but he didn't let go, his hands braced on either side of my bare arms. It occurred to me that he had yet to take off his gloves. I considered asking him why—though embarrassingly, it was only because I wondered what his skin would feel like against mine. If his palms burned now, would they set me aflame uncovered?

But something he'd said disturbed me more.

"Who says you are unworthy?"

He stared down at me, brows lowered. I couldn't help watching his mouth and the way he frowned. I decided I did not like it, that I preferred when he smiled, even if the things that came out of his mouth were frustrating.

"No one must say it for it to be true," he said.

"Then it can just as easily be false," I said.

"It isn't," said Lore.

His words frustrated me, and I looked away. "I cannot imagine why you would choose me," I said. "If we are speaking of worthiness, then I—"

"Your brothers are wrong," Lore said, interrupting. "It is they who are unworthy. They who do not deserve you."

"Just because you believe that doesn't make it so," I said.

We had stopped dancing, but the fae still moved around us, and I became highly aware of our proximity and the way I had to tilt my head all the way back to hold his gaze. I did not want to feel the desire curling in the bottom of my stomach. I did not want to like how his hands felt on me. I did not want to think about how his lips would feel pressed against mine.

Except that I wanted all those things. I just didn't trust Lore enough to give them.

His gaze shifted to my mouth.

"It seems we are at an impasse, wild one," he said.

"It would seem so," I said.

Slowly, the elven lord lifted his hand, and I took a deep breath as his fingers brushed lightly over my cheek.

"Come with me," he whispered. "I will show you your worthiness."

I closed my eyes, unable to face him. I desperately wanted to believe him. His words were familiar, like those that had called to me in my sleep.

"Samara," he whispered again.

His lips were so close to mine, I could feel their heat.

It rushed down my throat and warmed my chest. I held my breath, trying not to think about what it would be like to close the space between us, to press my lips to his, to tease this passion burning inside me.

And just when I was decided, a rapid clink broke us apart. I turned to find the dwarf from earlier tapping a spoon against a glass.

"His Majesty wishes to speak!" the dwarf declared, continuing to hit the goblet so hard, I thought it might break. Soon, he had drawn everyone's attention, and still the goblin king looked at me.

"Fae-kind," announced the old elf king. "The goblin king has chosen a bride!"

There was a mix of quiet murmuring and applause as everyone looked around in an attempt to guess who among them it would be.

I thought my heart might burst from my chest.

"It seems though that he is not alone," the old elf king said, drawing out the sound of every vowel in every word. "And another is vying for her hand."

A noise came from behind me that sounded a lot like a growl, then Lore stepped in front of me to block me from view.

"There is no competition," said Lore.

The goblin king stepped forward. "You know the rules, cursed prince. If you want to lay claim to my intended, then we must duel to the death."

I could not tell what I was more shocked by—that things had escalated to death so quickly or that these two were now arguing over who I belonged to.

"If you want to duel to the death, I am happy to oblige, but it will not be for this woman. She is already mine."

"Silence!" said the old elf king. "Intended, what say you? Which of these fae do you belong to?"

"Neither," I said, though I wondered if I had made a mistake, given what the fox had said about leaving betrothed tonight. "I belong to no one."

"If you belong to no one, then someone must take you," said the king.

"That is ridiculous," I said.

Another round of gasps, louder this time. I spoke over them.

"I am allowed more than two choices," I said.

"More than two? You want more than two men?" The old elf king's brows rose almost to his hairline, which had receded nearly to the middle of his head, though the crowd did not seem so opposed to that, their gasps morphing into more of an agreeable hum.

"I do not *want* anyone," I said.

"But you are wearing white," said the old elf king. "And you have apple blossoms in your hair."

I reached for the crown and pulled it off, tossing it to the ground.

The fae gasped, offended once again.

"What I wear says nothing about what I want," I said. At least I did not know it when I put on the dress or the floral crown.

Finally, there was silence after I spoke.

"I like you, mortal," said the old elf king. "If you will not choose a suitor, then you will reside here with me."

"Your Majesty—"

"You desired a third choice, and now you have it," said the old elf king. "Now, who will you choose?"

"This is obscene," said the fox. "This woman cannot choose between you three."

"And why not, Fox?" asked the old elf king. "Do you want to throw your hat in the ring?"

There were laughs, but they did not last long, for the fox spoke quickly.

"She cannot choose because she is in mourning, for her intended, a mortal prince, died this very day," said the fox. "It is only proper that she delay her choice for at least a year."

The fae muttered to one another, though I didn't catch what they were saying, hopeful that the fox's words had freed me from this terrible situation. Despite having accepted Prince Henry's proposal and my desire to kiss Lore, I did not want to marry. I wasn't sure I ever would.

"You make a good point, Fox," said the old elf king. "It is settled then. We shall delay for a year, at which point the maiden shall make her choice."

My relief dwindled.

With that, the music began again, and the revelry continued as if nothing had gone awry. I turned to Lore, who was scowling.

"Would I have been such a terrible choice?" he asked.

I was startled by his question but recovered quickly. "It has nothing to do with you," I said. "A true choice offers the option of freedom."

Lore's features softened.

"Apologies, wild one. It was all I could manage for you," said the fox as he trotted up.

"Do not apologize," I said. "I am grateful to you, Fox…but must I really return in a year?"

"Yes," he said. "You have entered into a bargain with the old elf king, and if you do not honor it, the forest will seek vengeance."

I frowned, feeling defeated, and looked at Lore. "Is the same true for debts?"

He studied me with a strange heat in his eyes. It reminded me of where we'd left off—too close and on the very edge of a great mistake.

I was glad I had not kissed him, or so I told myself as my eyes dropped to his lips.

"No one escapes what is owed," said Lore. "We all pay, with our time or with our life. There is nothing else."

I did not like his words, but that was not unusual. I disliked a lot of things that came out of his mouth, and I had only known him for a day.

"If that is the case, then I suppose we should be on our way," I said. "I would hate to waste more time."

I thought that Lore would be pleased that I had finally agreed to his demands, but his expression remained tense.

"My lady," said a voice.

I whirled to find the goblin king waiting.

Lore offered an unpleasant growl, which was growing far too common.

The half goblin ignored him, holding my gaze. "I respect your decision," he said. "Allow me to offer you a gift."

"Oh," I said. Again, I found myself in a situation I had never experienced before. It had been a long time since I'd been gifted anything that didn't turn out to be some sort of trick planned by my brothers.

The goblin king produced a small, black box that he opened to reveal a comb.

It was a fine piece of jewelry, made of gold and opal.

"May I?" he asked, taking it in hand.

I was very aware of Lore's gaze and also his anger, and I did not want to make it worse given that I now faced spending the next six days crossing the Enchanted Forest by his side.

"Allow me," I said, taking it from him and slipping it into my hair.

The goblin king's eyes were sad as he watched and then met my gaze. "Beautiful," he said. "Perhaps in a year, you will find your voice and sing for me."

"Perhaps," I said quietly, almost a whisper.

He smiled faintly before turning to leave, and I felt like I could breathe again, until I turned to Lore. His eyes focused intently on the comb in my hair.

"H-how does it look?" I asked.

"Terrible," he replied before he turned, stomping away into the darkness of the forest, leaving Fox and I behind.

"What did I do?" I asked, confused.

"Trust me when I say, wild one, absolutely nothing."

CHAPTER SIX
The Kingdom of Larkspur

LORE

A comb.

I gave her a knife, and she cut off my hand.

The goblin king gave her a comb, and she put it in her hair.

I stomped ahead of Samara and the fox, breaking branches and cutting down thorny vines. It allowed me to channel my frustration but also made the path easier to follow for Samara, who could not see like I could see in the dark.

What use was a comb? I thought.

It certainly was not as helpful as a knife, especially one that could cut anything in two, yet if I had given her a comb seven years ago, perhaps I would still have my hand and a shred of dignity among my six other brothers, who all found it immensely entertaining that I had given my beloved a weapon to use against me.

But they had not watched her toil in the mud and cold of a bog for hours. They had not heard how her brothers berated and belittled her. They'd not listened to her in the dead of night when she divulged her desires. They did not understand, because they had never sacrificed themselves for anyone or anything.

I could not wait until they fell in love, though it was rumored that Casamir, my seventh brother, had taken the beast we sent his way, the woman who had killed our sixth brother, as his bride.

She had been an angry and lonely thing, but she had fallen in love with him and broken his curse.

I was not so lucky.

Samara did not love me. She did not even know I was the one who had given her the knife. But she was the apple of my eye, and because of that, she was the only one who could make the wish that would free me from the curse of love.

"I know you are eager to find the wishing tree," said the fox, walking up beside me as I slayed another shrub. "But your lover is dead on her feet."

"Do not call her that," I snapped.

"Do not call her what, Prince? They shall both be true, one sooner than the other, depending on you."

I glared at the fox, but I could not help glancing over my shoulder to see her stumbling about, barely lifting her feet from the ground as she followed far behind me.

"She struggles, yet she says nothing," I said. "I cannot decide if she is brave or afraid."

"She is both, Prince," said the fox. "She does not tell you because she is not used to anyone caring about her pain."

"I am not her brothers."

"Right now, you are like them," said the fox. "You are angry with her, and since you left the elfin hill, you have pretended as though she does not exist."

There was no pretending.

I couldn't escape her. Even as she walked behind me, I knew she was there. I was attuned to every move she made—every small breath and every beat of her heart—but the fox was right. Shame poured over me, heavy and thick. I slowed beneath its weight until I stopped, turned, and went to her.

Her heavy eyes lifted to mine and widened as she came to a stop.

"I'll be quicker, I promise," she said, taking a step back.

The alarm in her voice was upsetting, because I had scared her. In the face of her fear, my frustration was not important.

"You do not have to be quick," I said. "Let me carry you."

"I do not want to be a burden," she said.

"You have been awake too long, and you need rest. We will not reach a safe place to stay for another few miles," I said, having already decided that I would venture into my brother's kingdom, the Kingdom of Larkspur. I dreaded the visit, but the fucker had soft beds and breakfast, two things I doubted Samara had in a long time. "Let me carry you."

I waited for her response, overwhelmed by the urge to touch her.

Finally, she nodded and held my gaze as I shifted closer. When I placed my hand on her back, she felt rigid.

"Be at ease, Samara," I said. "I am not angry with you."

"Perhaps not this second," she said. "But you are angry."

I said nothing, because that was true.

97

"Put your arms around my neck," I said as I bent and picked her up. Up until this moment, I had been able to mostly ignore the phantom pain shooting from my stump up my right arm in favor of my anger, but now it was all I could feel—that and the fact that Samara's face was only inches from mine. It made me think of how close I'd come to kissing her beneath the elfin hill, something I had dreamed about for seven long years.

Something that had cursed me for just as long.

Maybe holding her was a terrible idea.

"Are you okay?" she whispered.

My brows rose, surprised by her question. Looking at her now, I could not figure out why I'd been so angry with her.

"I am okay," I said. "Why do you ask, wild one?"

"Because you are staring," she said.

I smiled a little. "I am just admiring you."

She said nothing, but her expression was suspicious, as if she believed there was nothing about her to appreciate. I did not know how to help her see herself the way I did—beautiful and kind, someone worthy of more than I was even capable of giving.

"Sleep, Samara," I said. "I will take care of you."

She watched me for a few more minutes before closing her eyes, and I started our journey again, the fox trotting ahead. I was conflicted as I held her, torn between comfort and anguish. My body had yet to let go of the feeling she'd stirred up in the grove, and having her this close only brought everything rushing back.

I had wanted to kiss her, but I could not bring myself to do it, too afraid I would scare her away, but my greatest hesitancy was that she did not know who I was.

She did not know that I was the hand with the knife.

"In the grove under the elfin hill," she said.

Her voice sounded like a scream in the quiet night, and her eyes remained closed. I did not know if she could no longer keep them open or if she did not want to look at me as she spoke. My heart raced as I waited for the rest of her words, realizing that she too was thinking about the same thing.

She continued, "When we danced and you said my name…was that a spell?"

"A spell?" I was confused and also disappointed.

"Fox said that names have power," she explained. "When you said my name…I felt…like I had lost control."

I swallowed hard. I had felt that way since I met her.

"No," I said. "It was not a spell."

Her body felt heavier after that, as though she had finally given in to comfort.

There came a point in our journey when I turned from the fox's path toward the Kingdom of Larkspur, where Cardic, my second brother, ruled.

He was exactly as his name suggested—a dick.

"Prince! That is not our way," the fox said.

"It is our way now," I said. "We will rest for the night."

At least Samara would rest. I did not trust my brother enough to sleep in his territory.

"Are you certain, Prince?" asked the fox. "This will be unpleasant for you."

I was very aware, but as I held Samara in my arms, the desire to give her comfort exceeded mine. "I am certain."

Though with each step, the dread of our arrival grew and grew.

Ahead, I could see glimmering lights in the trees. They were the warmly lit windows and flickering lanterns of the fae who resided in Larkspur, the kingdom in the trees. A bridge marked the start of Cardic's realm, and I walked it as it twisted through the branches. It was a slow climb to his palace, past homes belonging to many kinds of fae—dryads but also wood elves, green men and goblins.

Something zipped past me, striking my face.

I knew what it was the moment I heard the distinct whir of their wings.

"Fucking pixies," I growled.

Cardic used their mischief and turned them into weapons. They attacked anything that came near him, even invited guests. He found it humorous, and the pixies enjoyed pleasing him, likely because they were in love with him.

I wondered what would happen if they discovered he was incapable of love.

Another pixie raced by. This time, I could feel her claws cut my face.

I ground my teeth as anger bloomed in my chest. I wanted to snatch them from the air and crush them into a nasty pulp, but as it turned out, I didn't have to, because as soon as another flew by, Fox jumped, capturing the pixie in his mouth.

He swallowed it whole.

That was the end of their attack.

Finally, Cardic's palace came into view. I was only relieved because my phantom limb had started to burn.

Despite having no fingers at all, I could feel the fire in each digit. I grit my teeth against the pain, as I usually did, and I started up the many steps leading to its entrance. His home was crafted and carved into a great, ancient oak that seemed to reach to the stars, vanishing into the darkness above. Over time, the sturdy branches had grown thicker and fuller, further encapsulating the stone facade of his castle. It had many open windows and great balconies, overrun with trailing vines and dangling moss, though to my great delight, I spotted a familiar vine with tear-shaped leaves. It was poison ivy.

I willed it to grow wilder, to creep into my brother's castle.

I hoped he would handle it and then pleasure himself.

It filled me with glee to think about the pain such a rash would cause him even as I approached the open, arched doorway of his castle for refuge. My legs and lungs burned, and I was hot and breathless, two things I despised unless I was having sex, something I had not done in a very long time, not since I had looked upon Samara. It was another side to the curse. I could be nothing but loyal to her. The very thought of fucking anyone else was… unimaginable. After tonight, I doubted we shared the same feeling. I wondered if she dreamed of the goblin king.

I held her tighter at the thought, my gaze falling to the comb he had given her. I wanted to pluck it from her hair and throw it into the dark abyss below my brother's kingdom.

"Do not do it, Prince," said the fox.

"How do you know what I am thinking?" I snapped.

"Because you growl more than me when you are angry," he replied.

I set my teeth, hoping to keep myself silent. Soon, we came to the final few steps, but before I could reach the top, something flew over my head.

I ducked and looked over my shoulder to see a dagger land and skid down the steps.

It seemed my brother had already been made aware of my arrival.

"You ill-bred, liver-eating bastard!" he shouted. "Give back my fucking fairy!"

"Shh!" I commanded as I lay against his steps, the edges digging into my ribs. I would right myself, but I was preparing for more daggers to be thrown my way.

"Are you...are you *shushing* me?" Cardic demanded. "On the steps of my own kingdom?"

"Shut up, you dull-headed, cunt-bitten coward," I said, my voice a raspy whisper. "Or you'll wake her!"

"Wake who, you spitting, ill-tempered fool?"

I peeked over the final step to see my brother at the entrance of his palace, cast in shadow from the bright light behind him.

"Swear you will throw nothing my way," I said. "For what I carry is precious."

"No," said Cardic.

I scoffed. "You are a dick."

"And you are a bore," he said.

"Fuck you, dick," I said.

There was silence.

"Are you quite finished cowering?"

"I am not *cowering*!"

"Yes, you are."

The comment came from the fox, who was sitting above my head on the top step.

"Fuck off, you miserable excuse for a cat. He should throw daggers at you. You're the one who ate his fairy!"

Suddenly, the fox made a strange sound, almost like a gulp. Then he began to cough until at last he heaved, and the pixie he had swallowed burst from his mouth. She landed a few feet away in a pool of yellow bile. She rose, coughing and sputtering, and then burst into tears before flying away.

"There is your pixie," said the fox. "Now, will you welcome us in? Your brother has been carrying his mortal for quite some time."

"His *mortal*?"

Finally, I rose to my feet with Samara in hand.

"What is *that*?" Cardic asked, as if he were disgusted by the sight of Samara.

I bared my teeth. "Watch your tone, dick."

"Is this the girl you have pined over for seven long years?" he asked, his amber-colored eyes sparking with delight. After a few minutes, however, a slow smile spread across his smug face. "The one who cut off your hand and never spoke to you again?"

I wanted to tear out his throat, but I decided against it. I did not want to chance the retaliation of his pixies with Samara so near. My scowl deepened, and Cardic began to laugh.

He laughed so hard, he bent at the waist, bracing his hands on his knees.

He laughed so long, he turned red in the face, and I thought he might suffocate.

To my great disappointment, he didn't, and he soon composed himself, wiping at the tears on his face.

"I can't believe I almost killed you and missed this," he said, still chuckling between words.

"You didn't almost kill me," I muttered as I stepped past him into his palace. I made myself at home, turning to the right and walking along a robust bough that acted as a floor. I ducked beneath low limbs and dodged clusters of leaves. Hanging among the branches were round beds, shrouded in sheer, gauzy fabric. I chose one closest to the ground since Samara could not fly and knelt to lay her on the soft mattress before covering her with a blanket.

As I did, the fox hopped onto the bed.

"What do you think you're doing, Fox?" I asked.

"I am going to rest, Prince," he said. "Be at ease. I am just a fox."

The creature curled up, resting his chin on his tail. I glowered, my eyes falling to Samara, who had slept so soundlessly from the moment I took her into my arms in the Enchanted Forest. I marveled at how peaceful she looked. This was her, unburdened by worry or fear, and it was beautiful.

I brushed a stray piece of her hair from her pretty, rosy lips, and then she sighed and turned her head away.

I glared at the fox.

"You had better just be a fox," I threatened.

He opened his eyes long enough to roll them and then went back to sleep.

I left, turning to find my brother watching.

"So how did you come into possession of her?" he asked.

I ignored him, making my way back down the hall.

"Did you slip her belladonna and steal her away?"

"I did not slip her belladonna, and I did not have to steal her away," I snapped. "I rescued her from thieves outside the Enchanted Forest."

Cardic pursed his lips. "Well, that isn't very exciting."

"Luckily, I do not exist for your entertainment."

"You exist for nothing, Lore, save this girl. Perhaps now that you have her, you can become interesting again."

I ignored him.

"You used to be an adept hunter," he continued. "Do you even remember how to string a bow?"

"Would you like a demonstration?" I asked. "I'll send an arrow right through your eye."

Cardic scoffed. "Even your insults have gotten dull."

I walked ahead of him, back through the foyer of his palace and into the adjacent hall. I started to open doors.

"What do you think you are doing?" Cardic demanded.

"Looking for wine," I said. "You have to have it here somewhere."

"Don't open that!"

But it was too late. The door was open, and I was surprised. I turned to my brother and pointed at the room.

"Why do you have a library?"

It was a nice library, with rows of floor-to-ceiling shelves and leather-bound books.

"Because I *read*," he said.

"Since when?" I asked. I had never seen Cardic with a book in my entire life, not even when we lived with Mother and Father in the Elder Kingdom.

"Since…a while," he said.

I narrowed my eyes, and he crossed his arms over his chest.

"I have hobbies, Lore. I am a multifaceted being."

"Multifaceted?" I asked. I'd never heard my brother use such a word in his entire life.

"You are just jealous because you are...*boring!*"

"And you said my insults were dull."

I looked at the library and then back at him, narrowing my eyes.

"Are you... Did you meet someone? Are you in love?"

"What?" Cardic asked. "No...no. I am most definitely not."

I raised a brow.

"Fuck off," he said, and I grinned as he walked past me. I turned to follow.

"So," I said. "Tell me about her."

"No," he said, throwing open a door on his left.

"So you *are* in love with someone?" I asked.

"I am not in love!"

"You are lying," said a voice.

Cardic had entered his study, where a jagged piece of mirror hung over the fireplace. It had once been whole and displayed in my father's grand hall, but before his death, he shattered it into seven pieces and declared that whichever brother assembled it first would be king.

Only one of our brothers cared about becoming king, and that was Silas, yet none of us wanted to give up our piece of the mirror because of its magic, which showed us anything we desired.

The downside was that the mirror also talked.

"Shut up!" Cardic said. "Or I will shatter you into a million pieces!"

"Shatter me," said the mirror. "I will merely speak a million times more."

"Has he asked to see her? This woman he desires?"

"Of course," said the mirror. "Just as you have asked to see yours."

It was true that I had asked the mirror to show me Samara, but in my defense, I was cursed.

"Why can't you keep secrets?" asked Cardic.

"Because I am a mirror," the mirror said.

"Show me this woman," I said.

"Don't—"

The mirror rippled and gave way to a scene that shocked me even more than the library. I expected Cardic's love interest to be…well, like him, immoral and unholy, but the woman in the mirror was the opposite.

"Are you in love with a nun?" I asked.

I was pretty sure the woman I was looking at was a nun. She wore a black frock with long sleeves and a cowl on her head. Every part of her was covered, even her ankles, and she was sitting!

"She is not a nun!" he snapped.

"She looks like a nun," I said. "She is wearing a veil."

"She is not a nun!"

"She is *praying*, for fuck's sake, Cardic! You cannot have a nun!"

"Don't tell me what I can and can't have, you self-rutting, churlish…*bastard*!" he yelled, and then he punched me in the face.

I heard the mirror sigh.

"I knew you didn't read!" I shouted as I charged at him. He swung at me again, but I grabbed his arm with my hand and turned away from him, bringing my other arm down hard on his elbow.

Cardic howled.

I shoved my knee into his stomach, but he caught my leg.

"I fucking read!" he said as he bit my thigh.

I screamed and then shoved him away. He fell to the floor. I pounced as he tried to get to his feet, grabbing his ankle to jerk him back. He collapsed to the ground and rolled as I climbed over him, my hand going for his neck.

I didn't even know if I could choke him with one hand, but I was going to try, and I didn't know why—because he refused to acknowledge that the woman he wanted was a nun?

I started to laugh.

I laughed so hard that I could no longer fight, and when my brother pushed me off him, I didn't care. I fell onto my back, still laughing.

"I'm glad my pain amuses you," he said, which only made everything much funnier, and though Cardic pouted, it wasn't long before he laughed too.

"I can't believe you're in love with a nun," I said.

"I can't believe you brought the woman you've pined after for seven years to my palace," said Cardic.

"I can't believe I have to bear witness to this," said the mirror.

We both glared at the glorified windowpane, but as we settled into silence, a different sort of emotion consumed me. It was heavier than sadness, worse than dread.

It was sort of like grief because the moment Samara partook of the golden apple and wished me free, I would have nothing, and I was just starting to realize that at least loving her from afar was *something*.

CHAPTER SEVEN
The Curse of True Love

SAMARA

I woke to something tickling my nose.

When I opened my eyes, I found three pixies staring back at me. I startled for a moment, surprised by their presence, and rose to my elbows, but they also seemed surprised and darted back, their small wings whirring behind them. They had large eyes and long pointed ears, both seeming too large for their small, delicate faces. Each of them wore a tattered-looking dress made of oak leaves. One wore the cap of an acorn as a hat.

"Hello," I said, though I was slightly apprehensive, wondering what sort of mischief they might intend, but before I could say anything else, the fox leapt into the air and captured them in his mouth.

"Fox!" I shrieked. "Let them go!"

I scrambled after him. I wasn't sure what I intended to do, perhaps shake him until he opened his mouth. I grabbed his tufted tail, but I wasn't prepared for the bed to sway. I fell forward, and he slipped out of my grip.

"Fox!" I growled as I followed him over the edge of the bed, where I found him crouched down, his mouth vibrating, as if the pixies were fighting to get out. "Spit them out!" I said.

The fox opened his mouth, and out flew the three pixies. I could hear their high-pitched voices but understood nothing as they zipped around my head before darting off.

Finally, in the quiet, I put my hands on my hips and glared down at the fox.

"That was horribly rude," I said.

He coughed, and blood sprayed the floor.

"Fox?" I asked, taking a step closer and kneeling.

He coughed again and then sneezed, shaking his head before sitting back and looking at me.

"If you think that was rude, then you don't know pixies," he said.

He licked his paw while scrubbing his face.

I studied him for a few seconds more before letting my attention drift to my surroundings. In the chaos of waking, I hadn't had time to think about where I might be, but now I saw that I was in a tree. Sunlight streamed in through the surrounding branches where round beds hung, some small, some large.

I had never seen anything so strange.

"Where are we?" I asked.

"We are in the Kingdom of Larkspur," said the fox. "In the palace of Cardic, the second brother."

"Lore's brother?" I asked.

"Unfortunately," replied the fox.

"Why?"

"Who can say what the Prince of Poison was thinking," said the fox. "But I suspect he thought you would be more comfortable sleeping in a bed than on the forest floor."

That was...thoughtful given that the last thing I remembered before drifting off was his anger. I lifted my hand to my hair, touching the comb the goblin king had given me.

"Keep it, wild one," said the fox. "You will need it."

I wanted to ask why exactly I would need a comb but decided against it. I was rarely ever given anything, and I did not want to throw away the gift from the goblin king anyway, even if it did upset Lore, which I still did not understand.

Would I have been such a terrible choice? he'd asked, but was it that he wanted to be my betrothed or that he wanted to ensure I would journey with him to the wishing tree?

Speaking of the Prince of Nightshade…

"Where is Lore?" I asked.

"Either dead or alive," said the fox. "Which, I do not know."

The fox's answer was unhelpful, but I suspected he knew that as he rose and trotted off down the hall. I followed him, entering what I guessed was the main entrance of Cardic's castle. It was beautiful. The walls were carved with intricate designs, with careful attention to the windows and doors, which were framed with leaves and flowers. A set of stairs was carved into the trunk, spiraling up and around. I craned my neck, wondering how far they went and what might dwell on the other levels of the palace, but dizziness overwhelmed me. I looked down, where the fox waited at my feet.

"Does Lore have a castle?" I asked, curious.

"He does," the fox confirmed.

"What does it look like?"

"I am certain I do not know," replied the fox.

I was surprised.

"If you have never been to his kingdom, how did you meet the prince?"

"We crossed paths while he was hunting. When he took aim at me, I asked him not to kill me, and in exchange, I would help him obtain his greatest desire."

I did not need to inquire after his greatest desire, because I already knew.

"Breaking the curse," I said.

The fox said nothing.

We continued down the adjacent hall. I considered shouting Lore's name, but that did not seem appropriate inside a castle, though neither did wandering around its halls without permission.

I paused at an open door to look for Lore but instead found rows of shelves that were packed from floor to ceiling with books. They were beautiful too, leather-bound with gilded spines. I had never seen so many. I took a step toward the room but stopped abruptly.

"What's wrong, wild one?"

"I don't want to intrude," I said, "or make anyone angry."

"They are just books," said the fox, skipping ahead.

I looked down the hall to see if anyone was coming before I stepped into the room. It smelled earthy and rich, and as I walked down one of the many aisles, I read the gilded titles and recognized none. I wondered what kind of books they were, if they belonged to the mortal world or the fae.

I started to reach for one, eager to hold it, to breathe in the scent of its pages, to read a story that would take me far from this place, when I heard a noise from somewhere in the room. It sounded like silverware clanking, which was odd given that this seemed to be a library.

I pulled my hand back and crept down the length of the aisle until I came to the end of the shelves, peeking around the corner to find a man sitting at a round table before a large set of arched windows. He looked like Lore but also didn't.

He was in the middle of biting into some kind of tart when he looked up at me, his eyes a stunning shade of amber.

When he saw me, he froze for a moment and then decided to bite into the tart anyway.

"You must be my brother's beast," he said as he chewed.

"I am not a beast," I said, stepping out from the cover of the shelves.

"I was talking to the fox," said the man. "Though perhaps I should be talking about you."

I did not know what to make of this man who was like Lore but also not.

"You must be Lore's brother," I said.

He rose from his chair and bowed, still holding the half-eaten tart in his hand.

"I am Cardic," he said. "Prince of Larkspur, the second brother."

My brows furrowed. "Why did you say that?"

"Say what?"

"Introduce yourself as the second brother?"

"Because the number designates our place in line," he replied. "Lore is the third brother, in case he did not tell you."

"To be king?"

"No, our father chose a different method for that. When we were together, it established who would eat first, who got the best horse, the nicest clothes. *Everything* other than the crown."

"And now that you are apart?"

"It reminds us of our resentment," he said, then gestured to a chair beside him. "Please, sit."

I hesitated and looked down at the fox, who was sitting patiently at my feet.

"Where is Lore?"

"Don't worry. When he discovers you are not in the bed where he left you, he will come looking for you. In the meantime, you should eat. I hear you have quite the journey ahead of you."

I shifted closer to the table. "You know about our journey?"

"Oh yes. You are going to break my brother's curse," Cardic said, though he was far more amused than I expected.

I sat down slowly. Cardic poured tea and then slid the cup and saucer closer to me.

"You...do not sound like you believe he is cursed?" I said.

Cardic held up a bowl in one hand and a pair of silver tongs. "Sugar?"

I hesitated, assuming he was ignoring my question.

"I...yes," I said. "Please."

He dropped a cube into my tea. "One or two?"

"One is plenty," I said. "Thank you."

"There is milk too," he said.

"Thank you," I said again. In the quiet that followed, I poured milk into my tea and stirred it with a polished spoon. Cardic was choosing pastries from a tiered tray.

"Do you like warm apples?" he asked.

"Yes," I said, thinking it strange that the Prince of Larkspur was serving me.

After a few seconds, he handed me a plate he had piled with fruits, sweet breads, cheeses, and meats.

"Thank you," I said again.

It was more food than I had ever seen in my life.

"You're welcome, beast," he said.

I looked down to see Fox again at my feet, and I bent to pick him up so that he could sit in my lap and share my food.

Cardic scowled. "Rats do not belong at the table."

"He is not a rat," I said, my tone bordering on terse. "He is a fox, and he is helping us on our journey."

The prince's mouth quirked. "Ah yes, the journey," he said. "To answer your question, I believe Lore thinks he is cursed."

"So…he isn't cursed?" I asked, confused.

Cardic shrugged. "Who is to say where love is concerned?"

"Love?" I asked.

"You do not know? He is cursed to be hopelessly in love with a woman who does not know he exists."

I could not describe the feeling that twisted through me, but it was violent. I dropped the piece of bread I'd just broken off. The fox was quick to devour it.

"What?"

"I see you did not know," said Cardic.

"He said he looked too long at an enchantress," I said. "I thought…I thought you could not lie."

"He isn't lying," said Cardic. "He fell in love at first sight."

"Why would he…not tell me?" I asked, but what

I really wondered was why he would almost kiss me beneath the elfin hill. Why had he spoken of admiration while he carried me to Cardic's kingdom so I could sleep in a soft bed?

"Because he is embarrassed," said the prince.

Well, that made two of us.

"Who is she? This woman he loves. Is she truly an enchantress?"

"None of us know," said Cardic. "But he has loved her for the last seven years."

I sat quietly as pressure built behind my eyes. I realized it was ridiculous. I had not known Lore for long, but he had been kind, and I was so alone, I'd let him stir up feelings inside me that I should have kept locked away. This was just another reminder that no one would ever love me—and how could they? As my brothers had often said, I was nothing.

"Eat, beast," said Cardic. "I know you are hungry."

But I did not feel so hungry now.

"Do you know much about the wishing tree?" I asked.

"I know as much as anyone," he said.

"Can more than one wish be made?"

"If you can manage to pluck another apple from the tree," said Cardic.

I frowned. "What do you mean?"

"They say it is guarded by a fierce raven with silver claws and a beak as sharp as a blade."

"Did Lore know this?" I asked.

"I imagine he did," said Cardic. "We all know it."

Except me. I wondered when he was going to tell me. More, I wondered what he expected of me when we reached the wishing tree. He had made it sound as simple as picking an apple. Now, that did not seem to be the case.

"Oh dear," said Cardic.

I shifted my gaze to his.

"Have I hurt your feelings, beast?" he asked.

"I do not think you care whether you have hurt my feelings or not," I said. "Much like your brother."

"That is quite a rude assumption," said Cardic.

I held his gaze. "Then tell me it is a lie," I challenged.

The prince narrowed his eyes, though a smile played on his lips.

"I see you have learned some things during your time in Fairyland," he said.

"Not enough," I said. I should have known to guard my heart against the fae.

"Well, this is quite cozy," Lore said from behind me.

I did not turn to look at him but gritted my teeth at the sound of his voice.

"You look terrible," said Cardic.

"Fuck you, dick," said Lore as he came to sit beside me.

I hated the awareness I had for him as he neared. Everything in my body went rigid—my back straightened, my thighs pressed together, and a dizzying heat swept through my body. I took a breath and worked to reel these feelings in, like yarn on a spindle, trying not to look at Lore, though it was impossible not to notice things about him when he sat right beside me.

The laces at the collar of his tunic were undone, exposing his chest, and his hair was mussed. It reminded me of how Michal looked in the morning after a night spent with one of the many women who warmed his bed.

A shock of jealousy tore through my chest, which only made me angrier.

There was an awful silence that settled between the four of us now that Lore had joined. He reached for a piece of bread. Instead of using a knife, he dragged it through the butter and then brought it to his mouth.

"Please continue," he said before he took a bite. "Do not let me interrupt your conversation."

I wondered how much he had heard but also decided I did not care.

"How did you sleep?"

It took me a moment to realize Lore was talking to me. I met his gaze reluctantly, growing frustrated by the look in his eyes. His expression was so tender. I had to wonder if it was all an act.

"Fine," I said, my answer short. I was too afraid to say more. I did not want my voice to quake or my eyes to water.

"Only fine?"

"What more do you want me to say?" I asked.

He studied me and frowned but did not answer.

Another bout of silence followed.

Cardic took a deep breath as if he were inhaling the most savory of scents. "Well, this is just *lovely*."

"Shut up," said Lore, his frustration obvious and a complete change from only a few seconds ago when he had inquired after my sleep.

"You shut up," said Cardic. "No one invited you to eat with us."

The two brothers glared at each other, and a different sort of tension built between them. It made my heart race. I recognized it as the calm before the storm—the quiet that settled thickly between me and my brothers before one of them snapped.

"Why do you hate each other?" I asked, relieved when my question ironically seemed to ease the tension between them.

Both brothers looked at me, but I kept my eyes on Cardic. It was easier to look at him, despite the fact that Lore's gaze was burning me up inside, as always.

"What is there to like?" asked Cardic.

"Surely, you can find something you like about each other," I said, though I could not deny that I was finding it hard to decide what I liked about either of them at this point.

"Can you find something you like about your brothers?" asked Lore.

I glared at him. His question *hurt*.

"At this moment, I like them more than you," I said.

Lore's eyes widened, and I thought that he looked a lot like I felt.

Good.

Cardic chuckled. "Oh, you are a beast indeed."

Lore's mouth tightened. "We were not raised to be siblings like mortals," he said. "We were raised to see each other as competition, to fight for the top despite the order in which we were born. *That* is why we hate each other."

I stared down at my uneaten food.

"Wild one," said the fox, breathless. "You are squeezing me to death."

I released him, unaware that I had been holding him so hard.

The fox expelled a heavy breath.

Just then, there was a sudden disturbance as several

pixies rushed in through the windows behind Cardic. The fox growled, but I held him close as they spoke in voices too high-pitched for me to understand, but I watched Cardic's and Lore's faces as they darkened with anger, and I knew something terrible had happened

They both rose to their feet at the same time.

"What's wrong?" I asked. "What happened?"

They exchanged a look and then left the table.

"Where are you going?" I demanded, rising with the fox in my arms.

I followed them as they headed down the hall and entered an adjacent room.

"Mirror, show us the three villains the pixies have seen," said Cardic.

Three villains? I held my breath as the mirror rippled, and a scene formed before me of my brothers—Hans, Michal, and Jackal. They appeared to be walking through the Enchanted Forest, where I could not say, though I assumed they were close if the pixies were warning Cardic.

I heard Lore growl.

"Do you know these three mortal men?" asked Cardic.

"They are my brothers," I said and looked at Lore. "I told you they would come for me."

"Do not fret," said Cardic. "They will not get past my pixies."

"Pixies will not stop them," I said. "They have hunted in this forest for seven long years, and nothing has harmed them yet."

Cardic looked at Lore and then asked, "What changed seven years ago?"

"They came into possession of a knife," I said. "A blade so sharp it could cut through bone."

As I spoke, I was unable to tear my eyes from the mirror as I watched my brothers stomp through the forest, their expressions equally terrifying and bloodthirsty.

Lore stepped in front of me, blocking my view.

"That's enough, Mirror," he said, and the image vanished.

I managed to hold his gaze.

"I will not let them hurt you."

"You cannot promise that," I said. "You cannot promise unless they are dead."

"I would have killed them before, but you begged me not to," said Lore. "Are you saying you have changed your mind?"

"Lore," I whispered, my eyes filling with tears.

Do not make me decide, I wanted to say.

"Your brothers might be hunters, but they are terrible at hunting you," said Cardic. "My pixies were able to lead them west. For now, they are ahead, and you are behind."

That gave me little relief. What happened when they discovered they had been deceived? I knew Jackal well enough. He was making a list of everything that was my fault and assigning an appropriate punishment.

"Perhaps, beast, it is time you become the hunter and they become the hunted," said Cardic.

"If they die, many will suffer," I said.

"And if they don't?" asked Lore.

"Then only I will suffer."

"Are these people you are trying to save worth all this pain?" asked Cardic.

"No," I admitted. It felt terrible to do so, but no one in that town had ever tried to save me, though they knew how horribly I was treated.

"Then why do you care if they live or die?"

"I care because I will be blamed," I said. "I care because if I am blamed, the people of Gnat will destroy my home."

I cared because my home was where my mother and father had lived and the only place where I could still feel their love, despite all the bad that had happened since their deaths.

The brothers were quiet for a few moments, but then Cardic was the first to speak.

"Perhaps it is good that you are going in search of the wishing tree," said Cardic. "By the time you reach it, I hope you will find the courage to wish that your brothers no longer exist."

CHAPTER EIGHT
The Nixie

SAMARA

I waited for Lore at the entrance to Cardic's palace with the fox at my feet.

I worried about what lay ahead, both because of my brothers and because I was about to be isolated with Lore as we crossed the Enchanted Forest on an errand to free him from the curse of true love.

My fingers curled into fists. I clenched my jaw so tight, it hurt.

He was in *love*. He was in love, and he had tried to kiss me. At least I thought he had. I could still feel the press of his forehead against mine, the warmth of his breath on my lips.

I could still hear the way he said my name.

It shivered through me and then heated me up, and I was *so* angry.

Ladies do not get angry, I thought. *Ladies do not get angry.*

Usually, my mother's words would quell my emotions, because I would remember how her warnings about my behavior made me feel—ashamed and embarrassed—and while I felt that way now, it wasn't because of my anger.

It was because of Lore.

"Goodbye, beast," said Cardic as he came to stand beside me.

I jumped, so lost in my thoughts, I hadn't heard him approach.

He smiled at me, though it was teasing. "I'll keep your bed warm in case you get bored of Lore."

"I'm not sure your nun would approve of you offering beds to young women," said Lore.

I turned to look at the prince who had suddenly appeared behind me. He looked more composed than earlier and now carried a linen bag, the strap across his chest.

"Did you just say nun?" I asked.

"Ignore him," said Cardic, glaring at his brother. "He knows not what he speaks."

"I appreciate your offer, Cardic," I said, looking at him again. "I will keep it in mind."

I ignored the low rumble that escaped Lore's mouth as I walked ahead of him, following the fox across the terrace, down the palace steps and the spiraling bridge as it descended through the boughs of other oaks, ash, and yew.

None of us spoke, not even as we left Larkspur and entered the Enchanted Forest.

"Where exactly are we going?" I asked Fox, trying to keep pace with him.

"We must continue through the forest and over the river until we find the witch of the wood," he said. "She has eyes everywhere and can tell us where the wishing tree will be."

"A witch?" I asked. "Are you certain a witch can be trusted?"

"It is not about trust, wild one," said the fox. "It is about the trade."

We continued, but I soon found it too difficult to keep up with Fox and fell behind, walking beside Lore. Our hands brushed, and I pulled mine away, blushing fiercely, though I wasn't sure why. I was frustrated with his closeness and how I couldn't stop *feeling* him. I knew he could walk faster than me and wondered why he wasn't.

"Did you mean what you said?" he asked.

I glanced at him. "What do you mean?"

"You told my brother you would consider his offer of a warm bed."

The crunch of our footsteps filled the silence as we passed over fallen limbs and scattered acorns.

"Does it matter?" I asked.

"Yes, it matters," he said.

"I don't know if I meant it," I said. "But I appreciated the offer nevertheless."

"You know it wasn't out of kindness that he offered," said Lore. "He did it to fuck with me."

"I do not need a reminder that I am being used," I said, stopping to glare at him. "I understand perfectly well I am a pawn in everyone's game."

"That is not what I meant," he said.

"I don't care what you meant," I said. "You talk

about your brother as if you are somehow different, but you are both the same."

Lore's features hardened. "Did I do something wrong?" He paused and then seemed to come to a realization. "What did Cardic tell you?"

"Nothing," I snapped, storming away.

"Samara!" Lore called after me, but I didn't stop. I continued forward, disappearing into the trees after the fox.

I had every intention of proceeding with my rampage, except that as I broke through the curtain of foliage, I couldn't move, and I found that the fox hadn't either. He sat, staring in horror at the same thing I was—dead animals dangling from the trees.

There were rabbits and deer, coyotes and boars, even foxes.

This was the work of my brothers.

"Samara, I—" Lore fell silent behind me. "What the *fuck*."

Panic erupted inside me in seconds, and all at once, the world was closing in on me. Everything blurred together, and I lost my ability to breathe, though I tried desperately. I nearly collapsed, but then Lore was in front of me, his hand on my face.

"Look at me," he said. "Look at me and breathe."

I couldn't.

My chest felt paralyzed, my throat swollen.

"Samara," Lore said. Dropping his hand to my forearm, he rested his forehead against mine as he had done in the meadow beneath the elfin hill. "You are safe," he whispered.

I had been so angry with him before this, but I was too afraid to be angry now.

I closed my eyes and managed a shaky, shallow breath. Then Lore wrapped his arms around me tight, as if he thought he could keep my body still, and I rested my head against his chest. I could hear his heart beating, an easy thrum. I wondered how he could be so calm before such horror, but it was likely not the first time he'd seen something so terrible. I had certainly butchered animals before under the orders of my brother, but this...this was different.

After some time, my breaths matched Lore's, and I felt less unsteady on my feet.

"My brothers did this," I said as I pulled away from him.

"I guessed as much," said Lore.

"Cardic said they were ahead," I said. "What if they circle back? What if—"

"Samara," said Lore, leaning forward to kiss my forehead. His lips were warm, and they lingered as he spoke against my skin. "I will *never* let them harm you again."

Now my heart was racing for a different reason.

He pulled away and slipped his hand in mine.

"We cannot linger here," he said, pulling me along.

I dug in my heels. "We cannot leave them like this, Lore."

"If we stay, there is a greater chance they will find us."

"Lore," I whispered, desperate. "This will haunt me."

I was sure that was what my brothers intended.

Lore stared down at me, his gaze hard and his jaw set. After a few seconds, he turned to observe the animals. It was evident they had been here for some time, because their blood had ceased to drip. All of it pooled on the ground beneath them.

"We do not have time to bury them," he said.

"Then we will lay them in a line on the ground," I said. "It is better than where they hang now."

He studied me for a minute, and I wondered what he was thinking. Perhaps he was trying to decide if he could live with disappointing me.

I hoped he couldn't.

"The moment I hear so much as a twig break or a pebble roll, we depart," he said. "No matter who is left."

I nodded vigorously in agreement.

Lore turned, and I watched him climb up the nearest tree as if it were a ladder, arms braced around the trunk, his toes digging into the bark. When he reached the first bough, he pulled himself up and walked gracefully along its length like it was nothing but flat ground. He stopped when he reached the first animal, a rabbit that twisted this way and that. Lore knelt and drew a knife. As soon as the blade touched the rope, it was severed, reminding me of the knife I was given seven years ago—likely the very one Jackal had used to carry out this massacre.

With the rope cut, the rabbit fell, hitting the ground with a grotesque thud. I covered my mouth with my hand, unprepared for the sound or the additional horror of watching these animals abused in death.

I knew my brothers were cruel. They often threatened to hurt Mouse and Rooster, but they usually took their anger out on me instead. Was this what happened when they couldn't?

My stomach revolted at the thought.

It wasn't until I tried to move the rabbit from where it landed that everything I'd eaten for breakfast came back up. I only made it a few steps before I vomited, my eyes blurry with tears.

This was horrible, and my brothers knew it.

They wanted me to feel responsible for each one of these deaths, and I did.

As I straightened, Lore handed me a waterskin.

"It's wine," he said. "But it will get the taste out."

I let the bitter drink flood my mouth before spitting it out, handing the container back to him.

"Perhaps you should pick some flowers," he suggested.

"I can do it," I said. "I want to help."

"Fox can move the bodies," he said.

I looked to see him already dragging the rabbit to the middle of the grove, and I felt my stomach revolt again.

Lore shuffled to the side to block my view.

"If we cannot bury them, at least they will have some kind of adornment," he said. "Flowers will help."

"Okay," I said.

"Don't go beyond the tree line," Lore warned. "And avoid the bell-shaped blooms. They are poisonous."

I nodded, and he returned to work. I tried to keep my back to him as I picked flowers, but I could still hear what was happening, and that was just as terrible.

When Lore was done and the bodies were lined up, he let me place the flowers on each rotting corpse. I did so with a knot in my throat, and when we were finished, we left without a word, continuing through the forest on our journey to a tree that did not exist.

I expected that we would travel late into the night, since the animals had taken most of our day, but when we came to a wide river, Lore stopped and began searching for a place to camp out of sight.

"Shouldn't we keep going?" I asked.

"Normally, I would say yes, but I am eager to bathe after handling dead flesh."

I swallowed, both at the mention of the animals and at the thought of Lore naked.

"You intend to bathe in the stream?" I asked.

He was bent at the waist, clearing leaves and branches from under an alcove of tree roots. He paused to look at me, amused. "Yes."

"Naked?"

"That tends to be how bathing works," he said. He was smiling more now.

I liked when he smiled. He almost looked like a different person.

"You should probably bathe too," he said.

My mouth dropped open. "Are you saying I smell?"

"No," Lore said.

"Yes," said the fox.

I glared at both of them. Lore glared at the fox.

"I am only telling the truth," Fox said as he sat with his tail curled around his feet. "If your brothers could not trace your tracks, they could follow your scent."

I turned away from them and sniffed myself, wrinkling my nose.

The fox was right. I needed a bath.

I wandered to the edge of the river. The shore was rocky, but the water was clear and grew darker toward the middle where it was deeper. I dipped my fingers into it and found that it was cool.

"Do not wade into the water alone," said the fox.

I jumped, not realizing he had wandered up beside me. I looked at him, confused.

"Why not?"

"The fae are not relegated to land," he said. "Some of the most vicious reside in water."

His words sent a shiver down my spine. I pulled my hand out of the water and straightened. It should not surprise me that the water, which appeared so serene, would actually be infested with nefarious fae.

"Then how are we supposed to bathe?"

"They will not bother you while the Prince of Nightshade is near," said the fox.

I turned to look for Lore and found that he had pulled a blanket from the bag he had packed at Cardic's and was attempting to secure it on a branch near the riverbank.

"What are you doing?" I asked.

"I am trying," he said, grunting as he struggled, "to give you…some privacy."

The blanket slipped and fell, half in the river and half on land.

"Fuck," Lore hissed.

I giggled as I went to him and picked the blanket up from the ground, wringing out the part that had landed in the water. I held it up by the corners and handed it to Lore.

"This will suffice," I said and started to remove my dress.

"I take it you've decided to bathe," he said from the other side of the blanket.

"I do not think I have a choice," I replied as I reached behind me to untie the laces at my back. I thought that they had been tied into a bow, but I found instead that they were in a tangle, and I had only made them worse. I dropped my chin to my chest, twisting both arms behind me, trying desperately to claw at the knot.

"Does it usually take you this long to undress?" asked Lore. "I am certain I could make quicker work of that dress."

"I do not want to hear about your conquests, Prince," I said, offering a frustrated growl.

Lore dropped the blanket.

"What are you doing?" I asked.

"My arms are tired, and you are not naked," he said. "Turn."

I glared at him, and he tilted his head back, looking over my head with squinted eyes.

"Is that a fly?"

He swatted at it.

"There's another!"

I scowled at him. "Fine!"

I turned, giving him my back. I wasn't sure why this made me feel so exposed. Maybe because I was about to wade into a river completely naked in front of a man, and I had never done anything like it before.

Lore was the first man who had ever kissed me, and he hadn't even touched my lips.

I wonder if he knew.

He could probably guess, given his years of experience.

"Thank you," I said.

"For what?" Lore asked.

"For letting me rest," I said. "You did not have to make yourself miserable. I am used to sleeping on the ground."

"You needed real rest," he said. "We still have five days of travel."

We were silent. I could feel him fiddling with the laces.

"Where did you sleep last night?" I asked.

I tried to keep my voice light, but I wasn't sure I succeeded.

His hand stilled. "What?"

My face grew hot, and I couldn't decide if I should abandon this line of questioning or plow ahead.

"Where did you sleep last night?" I repeated.

"I didn't sleep," he said.

My brows lowered as I considered the implication. "Oh."

"Why do you ask?"

"No reason," I said quickly, realizing how great a mistake this was. "I was just curious."

"Why are you curious about where I sleep?"

"I'm not," I said.

"But you just said you were curious about where I was last night," said Lore. "There must be a reason."

"There isn't," I said. "Have you finished? I thought you were adept at removing gowns."

"Samara."

I turned to face him, frustrated. "Because of the way you looked when you came into the library this morning."

He tilted his head to the side, the corner of his lips curved.

"And how did I look?"

I shook my head and shrugged my shoulders at the same time. I think the reaction was more for me—a kind of surrender. It was too late to back out now.

"Like you had slept with someone," I said.

"What makes you say that?" he asked.

"I *know* what men look like the morning after sex."

My face was so hot I could barely stand it. I was going to have to jump in the river just to cool down. Perhaps I would also drown, and then I could escape this humiliation.

Surprise flitted across Lore's face before he grew rigid with anger. He took a step forward. "How would you know that?"

"Do not condescend," I said. "I am not ignorant."

"I have never for a moment thought you ignorant," said Lore. "So you think I spent the night with someone?"

I tilted my head back, holding his gaze.

"And that bothers you?"

My eyes widened. "No, of course not."

"Then why did you ask at all?"

"I told you I was curious," I said.

"So you are saying if I *had* slept with someone, you wouldn't care?"

"No, I wouldn't," I said.

He stared at me, smirking.

"I think you are a liar, Samara of Gnat."

"Don't call me a liar!" I said and shoved him.

He stumbled back and fell into the river. The only problem was that I also fell, slipping on the roots at my feet.

I was barely able to hold my breath as I hit the water. Lore's arm fastened around my waist as he righted us and pushed us to the surface. I coughed and spit water from my mouth as it ran out of my nose before I smoothed my hands over my face and through my hair.

I found Lore standing over me, and I couldn't look away.

I forgot how imposing he could be, but in this

135

moment, there was no denying it. He towered over me. His tunic stuck to every muscle and made me realize just how broad his shoulders were. I wanted to touch him.

"You are most certainly a liar," he said, smoothing a strand of my hair behind my ear.

I closed my eyes at his touch, but it was not out of fear. A different emotion shuddered through me, and I swallowed hard before I looked at him again.

"Perhaps I am a liar," I said. "But what good comes from knowing the truth?"

Lore's finger trailed along my jaw to my chin. "I suppose that depends on how I feel about it."

"And how do you feel?"

He leaned close, his lips hovering so close to mine.

"I like it," he said. "I like it very much."

Then he kissed me.

It was soft, a slow press of his lips against mine, and when he broke away, his forehead rested against mine.

"And you?" he said, his voice a quiet whisper. "How do you feel about it?"

He pulled back to look into my eyes.

"I like it," I replied. "I like it very much."

Lore smiled and offered a breathless laugh.

His hand slipped into my hair as he kissed me again, longer this time. He shifted closer, our bodies flush. I let my hands move and twist into the fabric of his tunic. I didn't know what to hold on to or how to touch him. I hated that I was so aware of my inexperience when something this wonderful was happening, but I could not help feeling clumsy and awkward despite the heat surging through my body. I wondered if Lore could tell, if he thought I was terrible at this.

Then something changed, and Lore's arm tightened around my waist. He pulled me closer than before. His body was hard, and I gasped at the feel of him. I thought I'd felt desire before, but it was nothing compared to this. My body suddenly felt heavy, and I was desperate to be touched in places only I had explored.

I wrapped my arms around his neck. I wanted to be closer, even if it wasn't possible. The friction of his body provided a shred of relief as my breasts flattened against his chest and his arousal pressed against my stomach. I was no longer thinking about my inadequacies but how it would feel to have him inside me. I had never known such pleasure, and I had only dreamed of it with one person—the fae who had offered me a knife.

But all those feelings were ripped away from me as Lore abruptly ended the kiss and tore away from me. He took a few steps back, breathing hard.

"I'm sorry," I said, because I didn't know what else to say.

"Why?" he asked.

My eyes widened. I didn't really know why.

"I…didn't mean for this to happen," I said.

Lore's brows lowered. "What do you mean? You said you liked it."

"I did," I said. "I *do*. You're the one who stopped."

Now that I had distance from him, the cold reality of why he had stopped settled in. I crossed my arms over my chest, feeling exposed and terribly embarrassed.

"Why did you stop?"

"I had to," he said.

"Because you are in love?" I asked.

Surprise flitted across his face. "What?"

"Cardic told me," I said. "You are in love, and you think you are cursed."

"I *am* cursed," Lore snapped. "You do not know how I have suffered. This yearning…it has torn me apart."

"Yet you touched me," I said, my voice taking on a tone I didn't recognize. "You kissed *me*."

He just stared at me. I wanted him to feel as embarrassed as I did now that he knew I was aware of his secret, but instead, I thought he looked devastated, which I found even more infuriating.

"You aren't cursed, Lore, Prince of Nightshade," I said. "You are a coward."

I turned and climbed out of the river, using the half-drenched blanket to cover myself, trying hard to subdue the pressure building behind my eyes as I realized that my brothers were right.

No man would ever want someone like me.

Cold and wet, I curled up near the fox on the pallet Lore had made beneath the roots as quiet tears streamed down my face, and I eventually fell asleep.

———

I woke suddenly to the sound of music.

It was an airy melody, beautiful but haunting. I rolled onto my side and gazed out at the night, but there was nothing near as far as I could tell, save moonlight bouncing off the rippling river. I sat up and listened harder, realizing that someone was also singing.

There once was a girl with brambles in her hair.

Beauty they called her, she was so fair.
But she danced to music no one could hear,
Wounding her feet, which were small and bare.

I rose and followed the sound, my own bare feet sliding over stone as if it were nothing more than sand. I wandered down the river's edge, past large trees and small trees and shrubs with flowers so white, they seemed to glow in the night. The singing grew louder as I neared, and the foliage became denser. I was forced to elbow my way through thick shoots of green while the ground grew softer at my feet.

From quiet village to mountains gray,
Beneath starry sky and burning day.
The grass grew green where she bled,
And fairies followed where she led.

She danced until she wished to die
And came to a place where spirits lie.
Beneath that barren ground, there lay
Witches' bones and evil fae.

Soon a handsome prince walked along,
Drawn by the elves' silvery song.
So smitten was he with the dancing maid,
He promised to save her and drew his blade.

But when his feet brushed barren ground,
He began to spin and dance around.
The fairies clapped, their laughter rang,
Their voices rose, and they sang—

Finally, I pushed aside a curtain of greenery to spy the source of the singing. Two women sat on rocks in the middle of the river. One played a flute while the other sang and brushed her long yellow hair. They were lovely, dressed in white, and beneath the moon, they too seemed to glow.

The woman with the brush turned her head toward me and smiled, beckoning. She had strange features—large, round eyes and glittering scales on her temples. I thought that perhaps she was half human, but I was not afraid. I waded through the water toward them as she finished her song.

> *There once was a girl with thorns in her hair,*
> *Who danced to music no one could hear.*
> *And when a prince came along,*
> *He swore to save her, but he was wrong.*
> *They danced until their hearts gave out*
> *And died upon the barren ground.*

She paused and turned to the other woman.

"Look, Elke, we have brought our own beauty here," she said. "Perhaps we can make her dance." She turned her pale eyes to me. They were yellow in color and flickered like lantern lights. "Do you dance, beauty?"

I shook my head.

"Do not worry, beauty. We will teach you," she said. Slipping off the rock, she entered the water with me and brought her hand up to my face but did not touch me. "Beautiful," she said, and then she circled me, and I followed. The woman smiled. "Now we are dancing, beauty."

Then she took my hands and held them aloft, stepping into the left side of my body and then the right. I followed, unable to look away from her face. She was so beautiful, and her smile was so sweet.

"You are dancing, beauty," she said, leading me around in a circle, and then she let go of one of my hands. "Twirl."

I did as she commanded.

"Beautiful," she said when I faced her again, continuing to smile.

I smiled too.

"What…what are you?" I asked, spinning again at her direction.

The woman laughed, and it sounded like chimes. "Why, I am a nixie, and so is my sister," she said. "This river is our home."

"I do not have a home," I told her. "Well…not anymore."

"Poor beautiful creature," she said with a frown. "Elke and I will take you. Would you like that, beauty?"

Before I could answer, there was a terrible scream, and I looked to see the other nixie, who had been sitting on the rock, playing her flute, fall back into the water, a knife lodged in her eye socket. Then the woman in front of me hissed. My eyes connected with hers as she changed before my eyes, her teeth growing sharp and her hands webbed as she gripped my wrists.

"Mine!" she growled.

I screamed.

"Samara!"

Lore bellowed my name just as the creature yanked me into the water. I fought with her, clawing at her face as her hands fastened around my throat. Then suddenly, she was off me, and I was able to rise to my feet, choking on water as I gasped for breath and Lore fought with the monster.

"The comb, wild one!" said the fox. "Throw the comb!"

The comb? I had forgotten about the comb. I could

feel it in my hair, and though I had no idea how it might help, I obeyed the fox's orders, but it was so badly tangled, I couldn't get it free. I tore at the wet strands while Lore grappled with the snarling creature before me, but even he struggled. She was slippery and wet, but her grip was strong, and soon she was able to throw the Prince of Nightshade off with a guttural scream and dive into the water toward me.

Panic filled me as I yanked at the comb, ripping hair from my head in painful clumps. Finally, it tore free just as the monster broke the surface of the water and launched itself at me.

I threw the comb, and when it hit the water, it turned into a thousand spears. The nixie's glowing eyes widened, and she kicked her arms and feet as if she wished to swim away, but it was too late. She gave a short, high-pitched cry before she was impaled on the sharp spikes, and then there was silence, save for the sound of her blood dripping into the water.

In an instant, Lore was beside me, his hand on my face.

"Are you hurt?" he asked, but I really couldn't think, and I didn't answer him.

Instead, I turned to look at the nixie again, who was bent in half, a hundred spears piercing her body. Before, she had seemed to glow beneath the moonlight, but now her skin was dull, and her hair fell over her face in a cascade of yellow.

"Cut off the nixie's hair," said the fox. "And it will turn to gold."

I looked at the fox and then left Lore's side, wading to the nixie with the knife in her eye and pulled it free.

"Samara?"

I ignored Lore and went to the nixie with the yellow hair, took it into my hand, and cut it with his blade. As soon as the hairs were severed, they became glimmering, golden thread. I turned to Lore with his knife in one hand and the gold in the other.

"I'm fine," I answered, even though I was not, and gave him the knife.

I climbed out of the river and followed Fox back to camp.

CHAPTER NINE
Dreams Do Come True

LORE

I walked behind Samara as we made our way through the forest, pelted by icy rain. She was not fine, and she was cold, shivering so hard she could barely walk. I had tried to offer her my cloak, but she had shoved it off and left it on the ground, charging ahead wrapped in the wet blanket from the river. It was frustrating that she was so stubborn, that she would sacrifice her comfort just because she was angry with me.

I could fucking kill Cardic.

I would when I saw him next.

Why would he tell her I was in love when I could not tell her *she* was who I loved?

It didn't matter that she had kissed me back or that she had liked it. What mattered was that she did not know the truth of who I was, and I did not want to tell her, because I didn't want to watch as she realized her mistake and rejected me a second time.

She was right. I was a coward.

We continued to make our way through the forest, but soon even the fox slowed, his fur weighed down with ice.

"We must find shelter," I said.

"I know of a place," said the fox. "It is not much, but it is not far."

I did not care what it was so long as Samara was out of this weather.

The fox led us on, twisting through trees and down slippery hills until we came to what I could only describe as a lean-to. It was basically a room with three walls and a thatched roof, but it had an iron stove. Inside, the ash was nearly solid. I scraped it onto the floor, uncaring of the mess I made, highly aware of how deeply Samara was shivering. Once it was clean, I rose and headed out into the rain.

"Where are you going?" Samara asked.

It was the first time she had spoken to me since last night.

"To find wood for the fire," I said.

"It's raining," she said.

"There is still a chance I can find dry wood," I said. "I will return. Fox will keep you safe."

I wandered out again and searched high and low for dry wood. It was harder to find with the forest so wet, but there were dead branches tangled in the canopy above that had managed to stay mostly dry. I also gathered a few larger logs, as it was possible to split them into smaller, dryer pieces.

When I returned, I found Samara curled in the corner

and the fox lying on her feet. They were both shivering. I set to work with a sense of urgency, picking pieces of thatch from the roof to use as kindling. I pried apart the logs with my knife and shaved away pieces of dry wood.

Once a fire blazed in the stove, I turned to the opening of the lean-to and summoned my magic. Thorns sprouted from the wood, and vines burst from the ground, weaving through one another and blossoming until the lean-to was closed off from the outside. It wasn't necessary to keep the space warm, but I thought Samara might prefer it.

When I was finished, I turned to find her watching me.

"Sorry," she said and cleared her throat. "I just… haven't seen you use your magic before."

"I don't mind when you watch me," I said, even though she dropped her gaze after.

I took off my cloak and hung it from a knot on the wood and then pulled off my tunic, which was mostly dry, far dryer than Samara's wet blanket and dress.

"What are you doing?" she asked.

I looked at her, disliking how alarmed she sounded.

"You need to change into something dry," I said.

"But what about you?"

I smiled faintly. "While I would not mind you naked, I imagine you prefer otherwise."

She stared at me, then stood, slipping the wet blanket from her shoulders.

"Change in front of the fire," I said.

I took the blanket and tried my best to hang it so that it could dry while she changed. I wasn't prepared for how I would feel seeing her in my clothes. The tunic hung to her knees, and the collar was low, dipping between her breasts. I tried not to stare, but she noticed, because she gripped the front closed.

I cleared my throat and willed my cock to settle down, but my mind was already running wild with fantasies of how it would feel to have her legs wrapped tight around my waist while I buried myself deep inside her.

That was what I wanted, and that was what I would never have, which was why breaking this curse was so important.

"What happened to you?" she whispered.

Now I understood her expression a little better—she was alarmed by the scars on my body. I had a few lashes across my back, one of which curled around my shoulder to my chest.

"I was struck with a whip by a dullahan," I said, though a little reluctant to approach this subject.

"A dullahan?"

"It is a type of hobgoblin. They are nasty spirits who desire the taste of blood, but only from headless victims."

"And you encountered one?"

"I have encountered many," he said.

"Are there a lot here in the Enchanted Forest?" she asked.

I realized my mistake, and I did not want her to be afraid.

"Not really. I went looking for them," I said.

"Why would you go in search of a dullahan?"

I was quiet because the answer was…her. I went in search of them because the only time I never thought of her was when I was fighting for my life.

"Lore?"

"I'll take that," I said, changing the subject and reaching for her dress.

Once it was hung, I opened the satchel and pulled

148

out the only dry blanket we had and handed it to Samara. She took it and slipped it around her shoulders.

"If you sit near the stove, your hair will dry faster," I said.

She shifted closer as I sorted through the food I'd stolen from Cardic's pantry—dried meats, fruit, and bread. I organized everything on top of the satchel so Samara could graze.

When I was finished, I sat with my back against the wall and bit into a hard roll. I tried not to look at her, but it was difficult. My eyes drifted to her constantly. When she caught me staring, I looked away.

"Why do you not want to be in love?" she asked.

I clenched my jaw. My chest felt tight as I took a breath.

"I would not mind it if it was returned," I said.

She said nothing.

"Did you love the prince?" I asked.

"No," she said. "I had only just met him."

"But you agreed to marry him?"

"I agreed to leave with him and go to his kingdom," she said. "He told me he would give me time to fall in love with him, but once we were in the carriage, he said we were to be married once we arrived."

There was a part of me that was glad the thieves had stopped the carriage and a part of me that knew I wasn't being fair. I could not expect Samara to never fall in love. I could not expect her to never marry.

"So he lied," I said.

She nodded. "He said his brother had not returned from the Enchanted Forest, and he would have to leave to search for him. He was also looking for golden apples. It seems you are not the only one who desires to make a wish."

I was not surprised to hear it. I didn't think there was a person alive who did not want their greatest wish granted.

"What would you wish for?" I asked. "If you could do so without consequence?"

She shifted, drawing her knees to her chest. She looked so small and so frail, but I knew she was strong and unshakable.

"I would wish that no harm would ever come to Mouse and Rooster again."

"Mouse and Rooster?" I asked.

"Mouse is my cat, and Rooster is my stallion," she said. "My brothers are terrible to them just as they are to me."

It did not surprise me that she would think of others before herself.

"And what would you want for yourself?"

"I used to think that I wanted to be loved," she said. "But now I think that maybe love cannot exist without pain, and I have had enough of that."

"I don't think that is true," I said.

"If it isn't, then why are you wishing it away?" she asked.

I had no answer, and after a few quiet seconds, I cleared my throat. "You should get some rest. I am sorry I cannot give you a more comfortable place to sleep."

"It's all right," she replied. "I am used to the floor."

She folded the blanket in half and lay down.

I wrapped the food and put it aside so I could roll up the cloth satchel.

"Here," I said, sliding it under her head to use as a pillow.

"Thank you," she said.

Our eyes met and held for a few quiet moments. I wanted to kiss her so badly, the desire tightened my whole body, but I knew after what had occurred between us at the river that I would never have the chance to touch her again.

"Get some sleep," I said instead, returning to my place against the wall but I did not sleep.

———————

The next morning, the rain continued to come down in icy sheets and I let Samara sleep.

"Are you sure, prince?" asked Fox. "Staying will set us back another day."

"Do you want to venture out in this?" I asked. "As I recall, you could barely walk, your coat so weighed down with ice."

"I have no desire," said the fox as he circled his spot before laying down again.

It was a while before Samara rose and when she did, she sat up fast. I thought she might run, but her eyes darted around the small room until they found mine.

"Bad dream?" I asked.

She swallowed, shaking her head. "No, I…thought you left without me."

I was taken aback by her admission.

"That sounds like a bad dream to me," I said.

She frowned and then rubbed her eyes before speaking again.

"What time is it?"

"I believe it is well past noon," I said.

Her eyes widened. "Noon? Why didn't you wake me?"

She threw off her blanket and rose to her feet.

"If we were leaving today, I would have," I said. "But the weather has not changed, so I thought it best that you rest."

"Oh," she said. "But then you will only have—"

"Three days," I said. "I am aware but the journey is pointless if you die from the cold."

She settled again, taking her place in front of the fire, pulling the blanket around her shoulders.

"Thank you," she said.

The word set my teeth on edge, not because I didn't appreciate hearing it, but because choosing to stay was no grand act of kindness. It was required if we were going to have any chance at reaching the wishing tree.

"How did you sleep?" she asked.

I smiled a little. "I didn't."

She blushed, and I knew she was thinking of our conversation at the river.

"I'm sorry," she said.

"You are sorry for so many things and none of them are your doing," I said.

She dropped her gaze from mine, holding the blanket tighter.

"I suppose I am used to being blamed," she said.

"I am not blaming you," I said.

We were quiet after that, and Samara laid down again.

When I was certain she was asleep, I pulled off my gloves and then my prosthetic. It had been carved by dryads and given the illusion of realness by the blue fairy, but even with magic, it still made my limb hurt and sweat. A wave of relief I could not describe came over me as I removed the cloth layers I used to cushion my limb. It had hurt since yesterday, worse than usual because of the weather but I hadn't wanted to take my hand off earlier, too afraid I might fall asleep without it.

I sat, staring down at it, remembering the horror of losing it.

Nothing had prepared me. It had been there one day and was gone the next. I was initially shocked. The more I struggled with things that had once been simple—like using a knife to spread butter on bread or unsheathing my sword—the angrier I became, particularly because I could still *feel* my hand and all five fingers. At first, I tried desperately to keep it a secret, especially from my brothers, but in the end, they did not care that I lost my hand. They cared more about *how*, and the truth amused my brothers to no end.

I could handle that.

I could handle learning to live differently within my world. I could handle everything taking longer. It was the pain that made it hard, and it worsened throughout the day. It was like holding my fingers near a fire, drawing closer and closer until they were consumed, except it was all in my head, because I had no hand.

Even now, I kept my jaw tight as wave after wave of pain coursed down my arm, straight to the tips of my nonexistent fingers. I took a deep breath and closed my eyes, resting my head against the hard wall of the lean-to.

I don't know exactly what woke me, but when I opened my eyes, it was to Samara. For a brief second, I thought perhaps I was still dreaming, except that in my dreams, she never stared at me like this—her eyes wide with shock, her mouth parted as if she wanted to speak but had found no words.

Then I realized she was holding my hand, and that look on her face meant she knew exactly who I was.

"Samara," I said, sitting up. Inside, I felt frantic to explain myself.

"It's you," she said, dropping my hand and taking a step back. "You are the one who gave me the knife. I...I don't understand."

"Samara—"

She shook her head. "Why is it you?"

"Why not me?" I asked, though I didn't exactly know why. She had every right to ask, though in some ways, I felt defensive.

"Because you left!" she said, her eyes burning with anger and hurt. "You left seven years ago!"

I was surprised by her words, given she had cut my hand off.

"I never *left*," I said.

"You're lying, and if you're not, then I hate you," she said. "Where were you when I needed you? When I *wanted* you?"

Wanted me? When had she wanted me?

"I tried to help you," I said, rising to my feet. "Why do you think I gave you the knife?"

"You mean the knife that ruined my life?" she snapped.

"*Your* life?" A hot wave of anger erupted inside me, and I held up my arm to show her my hand was no longer there. "What about *my* life?"

She paled and averted her eyes before turning her back to me. I couldn't decide what her reaction meant. Was she ashamed, or did she find me repulsive? Though I abandoned that line of thinking quickly when she started to take off the tunic I had lent her for the night.

"What are you doing?" I demanded, though it was mostly because I was flustered, both because she was about to abandon me and because she was naked. She had undressed with little hesitancy, exposing her entire body to my starved eyes.

When I had first looked upon her, I'd never seen anyone so beautiful, and that remained true now, though it seemed wrong to be aroused in the middle of this fight. I tried hard to stay focused on her face, but my gaze slipped, especially when she turned around to throw my tunic at me. I caught it and dropped it on the floor.

It was the least interesting thing in this room.

"I am leaving," she said, turning to pick up her gown.

I drew nearer. She was like a flame, and the closer I got, the hotter I burned. I also didn't want to scare her.

"Samara," I said, hoping my voice sounded calm and quiet. "Look at me."

She froze. I didn't think she would listen, but maybe she was inclined because she felt vulnerable, cornered and naked before me.

That was not what I wanted, but I did want her to listen.

She straightened and looked up at me. I was so close to her, I could feel her breasts brush my chest as she breathed. It was sweet torture.

This will be my punishment when I die, I thought.

Or maybe it would be looking down into this beautiful face and seeing her eyes glistening with hurt.

"You left me," she said, and despite the threat of tears in her eyes, she spoke between gritted teeth.

"I thought that was what you wanted," I said. "You cut my fucking hand off!"

"Well, I didn't, you *fucking* idiot," she said. "Jackal

155

held my hand around the knife. It was he who took your hand and ruined your life."

I straightened, and she took a step back. "You think losing my hand ruined my life?"

She blinked, obviously feeling like that was the worst thing that could have happened to me.

"I could have borne losing my hand far easier if it wasn't for you," I said, inching toward her until she could go no farther, her back pressed into the wall, though she didn't look afraid. She looked angry. "You. You have stolen everything. I have had no peace since I looked upon your face. You haunt my every step. You linger in my dreams. I can do nothing without thinking about you, yet you say I have ruined *your* life!"

"I loved you!" she seethed, rising onto the tips of her toes. "I loved you, and you left me!"

For a few quiet seconds, I couldn't move or breathe. Her words had stunned me.

"You loved me?" I asked. I could not believe it. I needed her to say it again, but she didn't speak.

I shifted closer, though we hardly had any space.

"Do you still?" I asked. I was on the verge of panic.

"You were the only thing I had to look forward to," she said, her voice trembling.

"That isn't what I asked," I said, frustrated. "Do you still love me?"

The first tear trailed down her cheek, then another. I took her face between my hand and limb, brushing them away.

"I want to hate you," she whispered, her voice thick.

"*Do you love me?*" I asked again.

I recognized it was selfish of me to demand a

confession from her given the reason we were together, but I needed to know. I had to know.

She stared at me. There was so much between us—anger and frustration but also a deep and unyielding desire. I fought it now, on the very edge of breaking.

"Yes," she whispered, another stray tear sliding down her face. "I never stopped."

I kissed her.

I had dreamed of this moment for seven long years, and it had finally come. Everything inside me that had wound so tight suddenly unraveled. It was like a release of its own, heady and thrilling. It only deepened my desire.

I let my hand tighten in her hair as I bent over her, exploring her soft skin with the blunt end of my wrist. She did not seem to mind as I made a slow descent from her neck to her chest, to the swell of her breasts and the hard peaks of her nipples. She gasped, and it made my cock harder. I let my tongue ghost across her lips, teasing and testing, and when she did the same, I slipped into her mouth, groaning at the feel and taste of her.

She was exquisite.

I left her mouth to kiss along her jaw and down her throat to her breast. Her hands moved to my head, and I teased her nipple with my tongue and sucked it into my mouth. She let her head fall back against the wall as she inhaled sharply, whispering my name on an exhale.

Her fingers were so tightly woven into my hair, my scalp burned, but I didn't care. I would let her hold me like this forever if this was what I got in return.

I moved to her other breast, aware that she was moving beneath me, widening her stance. It was an invitation I took, letting my hand graze down her body to the back of her knee. I hiked her leg over my hip and then ground into her. The friction numbed my mind and set my entire body on fire.

I choked on a moan.

Fuck. I was so desperate to come it was embarrassing, but I had waited so long for this—for her.

I wasn't sure I could handle much more.

But then, the fox cleared his throat. The intrusion wouldn't have bothered me, though, if it wasn't for Samara, who froze instantly at the sound.

"If you two are going to fuck," he said, "at least wait until I am asleep."

I could have fucking killed him.

I probably would after our journey was done, except that now that he had broken through my haze, I was reminded of why Samara and I were together at all, and suddenly, I was consumed by guilt. How could I want this when I knew that I was cursed to love this woman?

I pulled away and met her gaze. Her cheeks were flushed, and her lips were swollen. I liked the look, and I liked more that I was responsible, even though I shouldn't.

"You should rest."

She tilted her head a little, raising a dark brow.

"You want me to rest when we have just found each other again?"

Found each other.

She said it as if she'd been searching for me this entire time, which had never occurred to me until now. My chest tightened at the thought, and I leaned forward to kiss her again before taking her hand and leading her to where she'd fallen asleep earlier before the stove.

On the way, I picked up my tunic and handed it to her.

"I'm not opposed to having you remain naked," I said, glancing at the fox, who was curled into a ball facing away from us. "But you might be more comfortable if you wear this."

I retrieved the blanket, a little disappointed when she decided to slip into the long shirt, even though I was the one who suggested it. Still, there was something so fucking beautiful about the way she looked in my clothes. It made me feel like she really was mine.

"Would you like me to spread the blanket?" she asked, her voice quiet.

I wondered if she was asking because I only had one hand or because I had been staring at her.

"I can do it," I said, shaking it out before letting it rest on the ground. I walked around to pull it flat. "I can do most things. Sometimes it just takes a little more time."

"I didn't mean to suggest—"

"I know," I said quickly. I met her gaze and held out my hand. She took it, and I helped her sit, though she didn't need it. She drew her knees to her chest, hugging them close. It felt like a barrier, and I wondered if she felt shy now and a little afraid of what the rest of the night might bring.

I knelt before her.

"You have never…lain with another before?" I asked. She shook her head.

"We do not have to do anything," I said. "I would be content to hold you until morning."

That was the most honorable thing I could do—the most right considering our circumstances.

"Maybe that is where we start," she said.

I nodded and then stretched out on my back while she lay on her side. Her head was on my chest, her hand on my stomach. If she grew bold and started to explore, she would find that I was aroused, my cock hard and heavy against my stomach. I doubted that would change between now and morning—or for the rest of this trip.

She was still to start, but then her fingers began to trace the faint scars on my skin.

"You never said why you went in search of the dullahan," she said.

I never said it because I dreaded telling her, but in this moment, I felt like a liar, so I told her the truth.

"I sought them out because I thought I could forget you."

She was quiet, her fingers slowly stopping their soft caress. I missed it.

"Am I so horrible to think about?" she asked.

"I wasn't trying to forget you because you were horrible," I said. "You are all I have thought about for the last seven years. I could not figure out where I went wrong, how I had managed to make you hate me so much that you would use my own knife against me. I thought it was part of the curse."

"I never hated you," she whispered.

I could tell she was close to crying again.

"My brothers grew suspicious, thinking my work seemed too easy, and followed me. They saw you give me the knife. They confronted me at the moor and forced me to give it to them. If I had known what Jackal intended…"

"I should have known it was nothing you were capable of," I said. "At the time, it made sense. I did not think anyone was capable of loving me."

She was quiet, but then she shifted onto her elbow and looked down at me.

"This cannot be real," she said. "I must have stumbled into a fairy ring when I ran from the carriage in the woods."

It was strange to hear her say what I was thinking.

"I can assure you, beloved, this is all very real," I said. I held her face in one hand, caressing her cheek. "The fae are too restless to maintain an illusion this long."

"Every day after you left was unbearable," she said.

"I shared in your misery," I said, brushing a stray piece of her hair behind her ear.

"I wish—"

She stopped short of speaking aloud, and I offered her a small smile.

"There is no undoing what has been done," I said. "I think all there is to do now is to forgive ourselves for what we did not know."

She shifted closer, her lips brushing over mine.

I held my breath to hold myself back. If anything more happened, I wanted her to lead. Then she slid her leg over my torso as she kissed me, and when she sat back, her heat settled over my sex. It felt glorious, even though I was clothed.

She froze, looking down at me, her hands on my chest. I rested mine under her knees.

"I have never done this before," she said. "But I feel like my body knows what to do."

"And what is that?" I asked.

We did not look away from each other as she moved, gliding over my cock. I tightened my hold on her, my hips rising, but she paused.

"Is this okay?" she whispered.

I swallowed hard. Of course it was fucking okay, I wanted to say, but all I managed was a nod.

She moved again, a slow pull forward and back.

It was the way she breathed that ignited me. The small gasp that came from somewhere deep in her throat. I tightened my grip under her knees and helped her move.

"Do you mind?" I asked.

Her eyes were dark and glittering as she shook her head, "No."

"Kiss me," I said.

She did as I commanded, and when our lips collided, I kissed her harder than before. We moved together, her hips grinding hard into mine. If I had been in control, I would have stopped to undress so I could feel her wet heat surrounding me, but there was too much momentum around what we were doing, and now all I wanted was to feel the pressure building at the base of my cock erupt.

"Have you ever come?" I asked.

I didn't know what she might have done alone in the dark, and I was curious.

"I...I don't know," she said, breathless.

"Do you touch yourself?" I asked.

"Yes."

Fuck. The bottom of my stomach tightened with her answer.

"Take off my tunic," I said.

She hesitated only a moment but did as I commanded.

"Fucking glorious," I said, squeezing one breast. My other arm remained behind her knee. "Now show me how you touch yourself."

Her fingers trailed to the curls between her thighs, but she stopped short of teasing herself. I wanted to put her on her back and suck her clit into my mouth, but I wasn't sure she was ready for something so forward.

"Kiss me again," I said instead, and when she bent down, I shifted my hands to her ass, gripping her as tight as I could, moving her over my cock. I felt her clit brush across the bottom of my stomach, and a delicious moan came from her mouth. The pleasure overwhelmed any reservations she might have had as she took the lead.

I watched her, awed by the beauty of this moment.

"Yes," I whispered, because the harder she chased her release, the faster she moved.

I lifted my hips higher and higher, ready to unwind.

The explosion hit like a physical blow. It was almost painful, the way my body tightened as it prepared to release another wave of pleasure.

When it was done, I opened my eyes and relaxed my jaw to find Samara staring down at me. I didn't know what to make of her expression. She looked flushed, and her eyes were glassy. Had she come? I was about to ask, but she spoke.

"Are you okay?"

I grinned. "I am more than okay," I said. "But how are you, beloved?"

"I am perfect," she whispered as she lay down beside me with her head on my chest.

In the quiet that followed, every rapturous feeling slowly left my body, replaced by guilt. I had let things go too far between us. It did not matter that she loved me or that my feelings for her over the last seven years felt real. The truth was my love for her was nothing more than a curse.

CHAPTER TEN
The Witch in
the Wood

SAMARA

"Samara," Lore said. His voice was near my ear, and his hand was on my shoulder. He nudged me gently as he spoke. "It's time to rise. We must be off."

"Go away," I said, burying my head under the blanket.

"Perhaps you should let her rest," said the fox. "You did keep her up half the night."

"Hold your tongue, Fox," Lore snapped before returning his attention to me.

"I agree with Fox," I mumbled. "Let me sleep."

"Has everyone forgotten that I too was up half the night?"

"Most men wouldn't complain," said the fox.

Lore growled.

"Don't you have a few rats to catch?" he snapped.

Suddenly, there was a sound like tearing vines, and a gust of cold air entered the small space.

"One would think you would be in a better mood

given your night," said the fox. "Perhaps you should listen to your *beloved*. I think you could use a nap."

I sat up as Fox leapt out of the lean-to and into the gray morning to hunt for his food.

"That wasn't very nice," I said, meeting Lore's gaze.

"You are only saying that because he wanted to let you sleep."

"What is so wrong with sleeping a while longer?" I asked, but then my gaze fell to his mouth, and I leaned close, my lips brushing his as I spoke. "Or perhaps you are eager for something else?"

"Samara," he said, though I couldn't place the tone of his voice. It was almost pained, but that didn't make sense, not after the night we had shared. I closed the distance between us and kissed him. I was too new to feel very confident in how I moved, but I liked the way his mouth felt against mine, so I kept going, soft and slow, but then Lore kissed me back, harder this time and longer before pulling away.

"This is wrong," he said.

I couldn't quite describe how his words made me feel, but I thought that perhaps my heart was close to breaking. My chest hurt.

"What did you say?" I whispered, meeting his violet-eyed gaze.

"Samara," he whispered, pleading. "What happened last night cannot happen again. This love I have for you, it is a curse."

I knew I was Lore's enchantress, the source of his suffering, his so-called curse, but I thought after last night, he would realize the truth—he had never been cursed at all.

"You think what you feel for me isn't real?" I asked.

He just stared at me.

165

"You don't want to say, do you? Because the curse doesn't make sense if the feelings are real."

"I know you want things to be different," he said. "But I have told you the truth from the start."

I shook my head in disbelief and then rose to my feet. I crossed the room to change, pulling off his tunic as I went and tossing it to the ground. I slipped into my dress, turning to him as I tied the laces at the back.

"I pity you, Lore of Nightshade," I said. "Everyone in your life who was ever supposed to love you abandoned you, but it has made you so afraid of love, you cannot even recognize it when it's true."

If he wanted to continue this journey, then I would do that just to prove him wrong. I would waste a wish on a curse he had conjured in his mind to protect his heart. I would do it because I loved him, because despite how much this hurt, I wanted him.

———

We left the little shed behind not long after our fight.

I followed the fox into the forest while Lore lingered behind. There was a strange tension between us. It was nothing like I'd experienced before—not exactly angry, not exactly desire. For my part, it was a buildup of all the things I wanted to say but knew he would not hear.

I realized our beginning was full of horror, that for seven years, he had thought I had rejected him in the most violent way and assumed his love was not returned, but I had suffered as he had suffered. There were times when I too thought I was cursed.

But I knew deception. I had lived with it daily since the deaths of my mother and father, and this was not it.

"What troubles you, wild one?" asked the fox.

I did not answer for a few seconds as we made our way over the slippery ground. There was a fine mist in the air that kept everything wet, but it was nothing compared to the icy rain from yesterday.

"Lore prefers to think he is cursed rather than accept that his love for me is real," I said.

"That is the nature of curses," said the fox.

"What do you mean?" I asked.

"Anything can be real if you believe hard enough," said fox.

I didn't like the fox's words. "So you are on his side?"

"I am on no one's side, wild one," he replied. "But it will take more than just your love to break Lore's belief. It is not just that he believes he is cursed. He believes he is unworthy of love."

My throat felt tight as a wave of emotion crashed through me. I had forgotten, but the memories returned now.

Who says you are unworthy? I had asked.

He had frowned as if he did not understand my question, as if it was a universal truth that the Prince of Nightshade was not deserving.

No one must say it for it to be true, he had replied.

"How do I make him feel worthy?" I asked.

"You cannot make anyone feel anything," said the fox.

"You are most unhelpful," I said.

"Why do you love Lore?" the fox asked instead.

At first, his question felt overwhelming as I thought of all the reasons, but then I considered how my love for him had only grown since entering the Enchanted Forest. How it had begun to burn hotter, fiercer than ever before, and I realized why.

"Because...he makes me feel safe," I said, and because of that, I had been able to let go of other feelings like fear. "How do I make him feel safe enough to love me?"

"I suppose," said the fox, "you just keep loving him."

We were silent after that as we continued through the forest, and it was not long before we came to a cottage with a pitched roof covered in thatch. A little fence surrounded it, and a path wound through a healthy garden to the door. I had never seen such a welcoming place.

Smoke rose from the chimney, and the air smelled like roasted pork. It made my mouth water, and I thought about how long it had been since I'd had a warm meal. My stomach growled, just as eager.

I started toward the house, surpassing Fox, when I felt something tug my skirt. It was the fox, who had taken hold of my hem to keep me back.

"Take heed, Samara," he said. "For we are in the presence of a witch. Do not trust your eyes."

A sliver of unease shivered down my spine and then moved through my entire body. At the fox's words, my gaze returned to the cottage, which was no longer so pleasant looking but cast in ruin. The roof was buckling, the garden was wilted, and the smoke smelled more like burning flesh.

In the yard between the house and the wood, a woman was bent at the waist, cutting grass with a sickle. Everything about her was gray, from her head to her toes, with the exception of a pair of black gloves. They reminded me of Lore's, though I doubted she wore them for the reasons he did.

"Do not speak in front of the witch," said the fox. "For if you do, she will refuse us refuge."

I had no trouble remaining silent or distant.

"Good woman," said the fox as he approached. She did not cease slicing blades of grass. "We are told you have eyes everywhere and know where the wishing tree will grow on the night of the first full moon."

"Of course, good fox," she said. Her words were cut with the snick of her sickle. "I can tell you where the wishing tree will appear on the night of the first full moon, but you must do me a favor, or none of you will ever leave this forest alive."

The hair on the back of my neck stood on end. Lore shifted closer to me, and I felt myself straighten.

"What favor, good woman?" asked the fox without fear.

"I have only a glass ax with which to chop wood and require a rick before morning. Go now and complete this errand, and I will tell you how to reach the wishing tree, but if you return the ax broken, you will die."

"I shall complete your task, good woman," said the fox. "But would you be willing to give my companions a place to sleep for the night?"

"I have only one bed," said the woman. "But the maiden may have it if she will help me cook, and the prince may sleep on the hay in the stables if he will cut this grass with my sickle."

"Thank you, good woman," said the fox.

She straightened stiffly and dropped the sickle on the ground.

"Follow me, pretty thing," she said.

Fear gripped me instantly, and Lore could not suppress his growl, which made the witch's face change. It was the briefest glimpse at her true self, a snarling creature with sharp teeth and eyes like pools of midnight oil.

"A moment, good woman," said the fox. "I want to say farewell to my companions for the night."

"A moment, of course," she said. "But then you are mine." She left then and entered her cottage.

Once she was inside, the fox turned to look at us. I wanted to beg not to be left alone with her, but the fox was quick to advise.

"You will survive the night if you listen to me. The woman will try to offer you food and drink, but do not take it, or you will fall into a deep sleep from which you will not wake." Then he looked at me. "Before you lay down to rest, stretch seven lengths of golden thread across the floor from the door to the bed."

I nodded and did not question why. After what happened to the nixie, I thought it best not to know.

"I will," I said.

"Good. I will see you at dawn."

The fox walked up to the glass ax which rested against the fence. There was a small clink as he took it into his mouth by the handle and trotted off toward the forest.

I watched until he vanished into the dark between the trees. When I turned, I found Lore watching me.

"I don't like this," he said.

I held his gaze. We were so close, our bodies almost touched.

"I will be okay so long as you are near," I said.

His brows lowered, and his mouth hardened. I did not understand how he could look at me this way, with so much emotion in his eyes, and still say what he felt for me wasn't real.

"I will keep you safe," he said, brushing his fingers along my cheek. His touch drew heat from the depths of my stomach, and I closed my eyes against it.

When I opened them again, my gaze slipped past Lore to the cottage where the witch looked out from her window, pale and hollow-eyed. Then I blinked, and she was gone.

"Samara?" Lore said, his voice hushed, as if he did not want for anyone else to hear. Perhaps he didn't.

"I should go," I said.

"Wait," he said, and pushed something into my hand. It was the golden thread.

"Thank you," I whispered as I slipped it into my pocket.

I stepped around him and headed toward the cottage, following the cobbled path as it twisted and turned through the garden. Like earlier, the cobbles at my feet were polished and new and the garden green and lush.

Do not trust your eyes, the fox had said, so I didn't and focused on other senses.

The cobbles beneath my feet felt broken and uneven, and the garden smelled musty and sweet. The cottage steps felt too soft and creaked beneath my feet. The handle of the door looked polished and shiny, but it felt rusty and rattled as I turned it.

When I entered the cottage, there was a lovely kitchen to the left and a small sitting area to the right. Everything appeared tidy and pristine. A fire blazed in the hearth before a long wooden table where there was an array of vegetables, potatoes, and pork, and though the cottage smelled like burning cedar, it could not mask the rancid smell of rotting meat or the pungent odor of spoiled potatoes.

"Come, pretty thing," said the witch from behind me.

I jumped at the sound of her voice and the feel of her gloved hand on my arm, which was slimy and cold, though it looked perfectly normal.

She pulled me into the kitchen. "Help me cook for your beloved, for that is what he is, is he not? Your beloved?"

I did not answer her, because the fox had said not to speak before her.

"There is an apron for you near the fire, pretty thing. Put it on!"

I did as she instructed, knowing it was not clean though it appeared bright and white. As I slipped the strap over my head, I was overwhelmed by a wave of nausea. If I made it through this evening without vomiting, it would be a miracle.

"Now, pretty thing, there is a knife and a board for cutting. Slice the carrots and the mushrooms, and chop the potatoes and the pork."

I approached the table. The knife she referred to was more like a cleaver, and when I took it into my hand, the handle felt oily. I dreaded knowing the truth, what horror it might be stained with. I started with the carrots, but the first turned to mush in my hand. Bile rose in my throat, and I swallowed it down, reaching for the second carefully. The mushrooms were slimy, the potatoes were covered in sprouts and soft, and the pork was sticky and foul. My nose burned with the smell of it, and I gritted my teeth hard to keep from retching.

"Now, pretty thing, there is a cauldron over the fire. Fill it with water."

The water came from a barrel near the hearth. I was hopeful that it might be fresh, but when I removed the lid, it smelled like rotten eggs. Still, I ladled bowl after bowl until the cauldron was full.

"While you wait for it to boil, pretty thing, you can clean the dishes and scrub the floor."

I crossed to the sink where stacks upon stacks of dishes were piled. I wondered where they had come from, though I suspected the witch had many visitors, and not all of them had a companion like the fox. I tried not to think about what happened to those unsuspecting guests, the ones who trusted their eyes and not their guts.

The dishes were tedious, but I was used to the chore. I took my time clearing the sink so I could fill it with water, which I boiled in a heavy teapot. My hands burned as I worked, but I didn't care. The scalding water made me feel a little better about all the horrible things I had touched within the witch's house, though it still smelled like sulfur.

At least the sink was near the window, and in my periphery, I could see Lore slicing away at the grass in the field. He was shirtless and sweating, his muscles and scars on full display.

I battled a wave of electrifying lust, but it was too late. My mind had already wandered to last night when he lay beneath me. I thought of how he felt against me and how desperately I had wanted him inside me. I crossed my legs as the ache grew worse, which only seemed to heighten my need, and in some ways, I suddenly understood why Lore might consider this feeling a curse.

My thoughts were shattered instantly when something sharp sliced me. I gasped and pulled my hand out quickly to find a cut along my palm. It bled heavily and stung as soon as it was exposed to the air.

"Oh, pretty thing, look what you did!" said the witch.

Her horrible hand latched onto my injured arm. I bit my tongue, wanting so badly to scream no as she dragged me from the sink. She brought me near the hearth and retrieved a canister from the mantel, smearing something jelly-like over my palm. I thought it looked like honey, but it smelled sour. When she was finished, she wrapped it with a piece of linen she pulled from her pocket.

I squeezed my fingers into a fist, my stomach churning, both from the pain and the anxiety of what exactly the witch had used on my wound.

"The water is boiling, pretty thing," said the witch. "You must add the meat and potatoes."

I did as she said and finished the dishes, even with my wounded hand, then added the carrots and mushrooms before scrubbing the floor.

By the time I was finished, the sun was setting outside.

The witch was at the hearth, ladling stew into a bowl, which she placed on a tray along with a loaf of bread and a bottle of wine.

"Take this to your beloved," she said. "Be sure he does not leave a drop, and when you return, you may have some of your own."

I was suspicious of her instructions but relieved at the same time. I took the tray and carried it to the door. The smell of the stew made my stomach turn. Saliva gathered in my mouth, and I knew I was going to vomit. Thankfully, as soon as I was outside the cottage, the cold air washed over me, and the feeling lessened. I paused on the rotting step and took a deep breath before following the cobblestone path from the garden.

Lore was no longer in the field. I found him in the

stables, having just spread a blanket on the hay-covered floor. He was still shirtless, still sweaty from his work in the field. He had tied his hair back, and the angles of his face looked just as fierce as his eyes, which raked down my body.

"Are you okay?" he asked.

I nodded, dropping my gaze to the tray. "I know Fox said not to accept food and drink," I said. "But the witch instructed me to bring you dinner. I thought perhaps we could share what food we already had."

"Of course," Lore said.

I set the tray down on a nearby barrel. When I turned to face Lore again, his eyes were on my hand.

"I thought you said you were okay," he said.

"I am," I said. "Mostly."

He crossed to me and took my hand, unwinding the bandage. He bent to smell the salve.

"I don't know what she used on it," I said.

"Nothing that will heal, certainly," he said. "Sit, and I will dress it."

I obeyed, only realizing now how badly my feet hurt. Lore retrieved the satchel and then came to kneel in front of me.

"How do you think Fox fares in the forest?" I asked.

"I am sure he is fine," said Lore. "Hold out your hand."

I did as he said. He scraped away what remained of the witch's medicine and then pulled the waterskin from the satchel and poured fresh water over the wound, squeezing it until it bled.

The pain was almost like being cut again, and I inhaled a breath between my teeth.

"I'm sorry," he said. "I just want to make sure it is clean."

"I know. It's okay," I said.

175

After he seemed satisfied with the cleansing, he placed his hand over a patch of ground, and beneath it sprouted a green stem with pointed leaves and berries that looked almost like black tomatoes.

"What is that?" I asked.

"It is called deadly nightshade," said Lore.

He let the plant grow until it was a few inches tall before he ripped it from the ground and then tore the leaves free, leaving only the stems, from which he squeezed a pulp-like salve onto the cut. When he was finished, he tore a strip of cloth from his tunic and wrapped it around my hand.

"Before you leave, I'll replace the witch's rag," said Lore. "She will be none the wiser."

The thought of returning to that awful cottage filled me with dread. "Do you think she will know if I do not go back?"

"We risk offending her if we do not do as she says," he said.

"She expects me to eat when I go back inside," I said.

"Then we will make it appear as though you have eaten with me," Lore said, handing me a piece of bread from our own supplies.

I took it, but I wasn't very hungry. The smell of rancid meat lingered in my nose, which meant I could also taste it in the back of my throat.

I ate the bread and then reached into the satchel for the other waterskin, which was full of wine. I downed a mouthful and then another. When I was finished, I found Lore watching me.

"I can't escape what I have seen and felt in that cottage," I said. "Everything looks pretty and clean, but my body tells me otherwise."

"If I could, I would take your place," he said. "But I suspect the witch does not like fae, especially elvish princes."

"I will be fine," I said, looking down at my hands. "I would do anything for you."

Slowly, I raised my head and met his gaze. My heart beat faster as I thought about the words I was going to say. Then they started to tumble out of my mouth, and they fell into the air between us where I could not take them back.

"You may think you are cursed," I said. "But my love for you is very real."

"Samara." My name slipped from Lore's mouth in a pained whisper. "Please, Samara."

"In two days, I will partake of the golden apple and wish you free of your love for me, but I will still love you. I will always love you. I deserve to know what it's like to be loved by you before it is too late."

My voice trembled. I could not tell if it was from anger or sadness. I felt overwhelmed by both at this moment. I rose to my knees and unlaced my dress, pulling it over my head and casting it aside. I sat there, kneeling naked before the prince I had loved for seven long years, waiting for him to say something—anything.

He stared at me, mouth tense.

Just when I started to think he would do nothing, the word *coward* poised on the tip of my tongue, he was on his knees in front of me. His hand tangled in my hair, and he guided my head back so he could look into my eyes.

"I always dreamed this moment would happen somewhere far nicer than the floor of a stable," he said. "You deserve more than this."

"I don't need anything else," I said. "I just need you."

He stared at me a few seconds longer. I think he was looking for any sign of doubt, but I had none. I had never taken what I wanted, but I was going to tonight.

I kissed him, and his hesitation fell away as his fingers fisted in my hair. My lips parted on a moan, and his tongue slid against my own, teasing before he kissed me long and slow and deep. My heart beat rapidly as my hands moved to his chest. I tried to guide him to his back, because all I knew was what we had done last night, but Lore stopped me, smiling as he broke our kiss.

"Be patient, beloved," he said. Tilting my head back, he brushed his thumb over the curve of my swollen lips. "I have plans for you."

I liked the look in his eyes. It was hunger, gnawing and deep. The kind that made you feel hollow. I had seen it in his gaze before but to a lesser degree. Tonight, it roared to life, and a thrill shivered through me, knowing that I was what he craved.

"I…don't know what to do," I said.

I didn't need to say it, but I felt like I had to provide some kind of excuse in case I was terrible.

"Samara," he said, resting his forehead against mine. "You are perfect."

He kissed me again and then guided me to my back. He didn't follow but stayed seated on his heels, staring down at me. I felt exposed and moved to cover myself, turning my knee slightly into the other, as if I could hide from Lore, whose eyes only darkened at the sight.

"I will have my face there soon enough," he said. "You might as well let me look."

"It is an easy request for someone who is still clothed."

The corner of his mouth lifted, but I knew by the

gleam in his eyes he had taken my words as a challenge. I lifted myself onto my elbows as he rose to his feet and unlaced his trousers, pulling them off. As he straightened, my eyes roamed over his body but stopped at his arousal, which was thick and rigid. I blushed fiercely when I realized it was the only thing I was staring at, but I was also thinking about what it would feel like to have him inside me soon.

I don't know what possessed me. Perhaps it was just the way he was looking at me now, but I shifted to my knees again, my face level with his sex. I lifted my hand but didn't touch him, moving my gaze to his. I suppose I wanted permission.

"You can touch me." His voice was strained. I wondered if he felt like I had felt all day—wound so tight, I could barely breathe.

I turned my attention to his arousal and let my fingers drift from the crown of his cock to the bottom where his balls hung heavy between his thighs. He was soft, which surprised me. No other part of his body felt like this.

"Will I hurt you?" I asked.

"I will tell you," he said. "Wrap your fingers around me."

I did as he said, and then he wrapped his own around mine and moved my hand up and down, letting out a low breath as I followed his lead.

"And that feels good?"

"Yes," he said, breathless. "Very."

"What else do I do?" I asked.

Again, Lore let out another long breath.

"Sweet Samara," he said, and I was surprised when he pulled my hand away from him and then knelt in front of me. "Let me show you how good this can be for you."

"I want to please you," I said.

I did not want to bring up my brothers, but I knew how they talked about the women who frequented our cottage. I knew who had satisfied them and who didn't.

"Beloved, you please me simply by existing," he said.

He kissed me long and slow, guiding me until I rested on my back again. He remained upright, staring down at me.

"You are so fucking beautiful," he said, and then he placed his knee between my legs, nudging them apart. He settled into that space and then rested his elbows on either side of my head, continuing our kiss. At some point, he let himself relax fully and my breath caught in my throat. He was so warm, and his arousal settled against my heat, heavy and hard. I wanted to be full of him, and I reacted without thought, widening my legs and lifting my hips.

Lore groaned against my mouth and then dragged his lips along my jaw and neck. He trailed kisses down my chest, between my breasts, before taking each into his mouth in turn. He teased mercilessly, plying my nipples with his tongue and then sucking hard. It was a push and pull of overwhelming pleasure and dizzying relief.

I had some idea of what he intended as he pressed soft kisses down my stomach, but it was another matter entirely once he arrived at the apex of my thighs. The inclination to press my knees together overwhelmed me, but Lore was there, and he was looking at a part of me no one ever had like he looked at all of me—as if it was the most beautiful thing in the world.

He kissed the inside of my thigh as he met my gaze, and I swallowed hard as a fierce blush stained my cheeks.

"You are perfect," he said.

He continued kissing along my thigh and then the other before settling completely on his stomach and kissing my heat. He did it again, harder this time, burying his face between the soft mound of curls between my legs.

I gasped, pressing my head into the floor.

I didn't know what to do with my hands. At first, I let them twist into his hair. It felt safe because if I grew too insecure, I could pull him away, but then he used his fingers to part my flesh and licked along my heat, letting his tongue circle where I ached most. I let out a moan, my head falling back.

Lore pulled away. "Is it good?" he asked.

"Yes," I breathed. My eyes were closed, and my chest rose and fell heavily. I had held my breath the entire time. "Yes."

He licked me again, and then his mouth closed over my clit. He sucked gently, and I thought I might die. I dug my heels into the floor but couldn't go anywhere, because Lore's arms were locked around my legs to keep me still, his face pressing harder into my sex.

When he let me go, he exhaled deeply, and when I looked at him, his lips were wet with my arousal. A wave of embarrassment burned through my body, but the corner of Lore's mouth lifted, his eyes dark with lust.

"There is no room for shame here, beloved," he said. "It's okay to love this. I do."

He turned his attention to me again. This time, his fingers trailed along my opening, deepening as he moved through my heat until one finger slipped fully inside. I instinctively tightened at the invasion, but then his mouth was on me again, and I was able to relax. Soon I felt molten, and he slipped another finger inside. The muscles in the bottom of my stomach contracted, and I gripped Lore between my thighs, unable to do anything else. It felt instinctual, and it gave me what I wanted, heightening the pressure and pleasure in a way I hadn't felt before.

Lore pulled away long enough to let out a low curse. Then he was back, but this time with a steady and unending rhythm. His fingers curled inside me while he licked and sucked my clit, and my legs pressed into him so hard, I shook. Inside, I was rising higher and higher, the pleasure moving from the depths of my stomach straight to my head until it unraveled.

The cry that left my mouth scraped against my throat. I could not even open my eyes. It felt like my body had pulled everything inside me to a single point between my thighs. If it wasn't so pleasurable, it would have been painful. I curled into myself as tremor after tremor shook my entire body. When it lessened, I could relax, but my eyes were heavy.

He had taken all my strength in a matter of seconds.

I heard him chuckle, and I opened my eyes enough to see his smug expression.

He was proud of himself.

He kissed the inside of my knee.

"How did that feel?" he asked.

"You know how it felt, arrogant prince," I said. "Is it a requirement to praise your mouth before we continue?"

He grinned and then shifted, resting one elbow, then the other on either side of my stomach. He kissed his way up my body. I felt warm and relaxed. I felt ready for him, even surer when his cock came to rest against my wet heat.

As quickly as he had brought me to release, the desire ignited again. It was a strange type of torture but one I was desperate for.

I held Lore's gaze as he brushed strands of hair from my face.

"I love you," I said, unable to bring my voice above a whisper. I was a little afraid he would recoil at my words, but his expression only grew softer.

"What I have felt for you these last seven years, it borders on obsession. I have never felt anything like it. I never will again."

I was surprised by his words but also confused. It was a confession of his feelings for me but also an acknowledgement that it would end.

He kissed me though, and I was reminded of why I had made this decision. I loved Lore despite everything, and this was what it was like to be loved by him.

When he pulled away, he let his nose drift down mine.

"Are you ready?" he asked.

I nodded, because I couldn't speak.

He shifted his weight to one side, reaching between us to guide the head of his cock through my heat before resting his forearms on either side of my head.

We were both a little breathless, though nothing had happened yet.

He kissed me again, once hard and deep, once soft and slow, and as he broke from my lips, he rocked his hips into mine. I let out a breath. There was no pain but a sweet pressure, and I widened my legs preparing to take more of him, though I found it difficult to relax. The anticipation kept me rigid, my heels were pressed into the floor, my back arched into him.

He kissed my forehead, one of his arms resting beneath my head.

"Wrap your legs around my waist," he said.

I followed his instructions, and the tension in my body lessened, then he drove into me again, this time to the hilt. I took in a sharp breath, but not because it hurt. It was because I was surprised.

Lore kissed my face and my neck and told me to breathe. I held his gaze. I had dreamed of so many aspects of what this moment would be like, but the one I could never have imagined was how close I would feel to him. This went beyond the way our bodies were connected. It was another level of existence, and within this space, I knew I would never love another as long as I lived.

"How do you feel?" he asked.

"Like I am dreaming," I said, slipping his hair behind his ear. "You?"

He gave a breathless laugh. "I feel like I might die if I do not move soon."

"I'm ready," I said.

He studied me, kissed me again.

"You are everything," he said.

His words twisted inside me. They were so close to the ones I wanted to hear but still so far away, but there came a point after he started to move that I no longer cared how he told me he loved me, because I could feel it in every part of my body. It was like he had taken ahold of everything inside me. My head fell back, and my hands slid over his back to his ass. I gripped him hard and pulled him into me. I wanted as much of him as I could get.

"Samara," he whispered my name as he kissed along my throat, matching the pace I desired. "Beloved."

He buried his face in the crook of my neck and held me tight as he rocked into me over and over, faster and faster, until his breath caught hard in his throat and his entire body tensed as he came. I could not describe the euphoria I felt, knowing that part of him was inside me, and I knew I'd been right to ask for this.

"Are you okay?" he asked as his body relaxed against mine.

"Yes," I said. "I am perfect."

"There is nothing truer," he said, his lips teasing mine.

We kissed and explored each other in the aftermath of our coupling, but there came a point when I knew I had to go. It was strange rising from where we had made love. I felt different, renewed in a way I never expected, and so in love my heart ached.

Once I was dressed, I turned to find Lore watching me. His stare was hard, and his brows were lowered. My heart ached suddenly, afraid that he had already decided to regret what happened between us. I decided I wouldn't ask, because I didn't want to know. I would show him soon enough that we were meant to be together, that his love for me was just as real as what we had shared tonight.

"Here," he said, wrapping the witch's ragged bandage around my hand to hide his work. After, he picked up the bowl of stew. "Rub some of the juice around your mouth, and pour it on your apron. I know it will be awful, but she will think you have eaten with me."

I took the bowl in hand, but before I could complete the task, Lore tilted my head back, and his mouth came down upon mine. I wanted so badly to stay with him, but there would be other nights, I told myself, knowing I was trading this one for hundreds more after.

"Get some sleep, wild one," Lore whispered when he pulled away.

I held my breath as I smeared the horrible stew around my mouth and poured it on the apron the witch had given me before leaving the barn. I paused at the door to look back at Lore.

"I love you," I said, because I did not think I could say it enough, but I turned before I could see his expression and hurried to the witch's cottage where a pretty orange glow filled the windows, though I knew it to be from the fire upon which the rancid stew still boiled—and likely many other terrible things.

I tried to prepare myself for what I would hear and taste and smell on the other side of her rotten door, but knowing what to expect did not make it any easier.

I cringed, turning the rusty knob, and a wave of nausea hit as I pushed the squealing door open. The witch was sitting in a chair, rocking back and forth, knitting with a pair of long needles. As she worked, they scraped against each other, and I ground my teeth harder and harder with each pass.

"You have been gone for quite some time, pretty thing," said the witch. "Your dinner has gone cold."

I glanced at the table and saw that she had prepared my bowl. There was a glass of wine and a loaf of bread too. When my gaze returned to the witch, she had moved and stood only an inch from me. I was glad that I'd clenched my jaw so tight. It kept me from screaming at her nearness, but I did stagger back. She gripped my wrist as she seemed fond of doing and dragged me close, taking a deep breath.

"You smell like the prince," she said. "But it seems

you are full. Full of the prince and full of stew. Now it is off to bed with you."

She turned and dragged me into the dark of her cottage, to a room with an iron bed. It was neatly made, with many pillows and a coverlet edged with lace. A candle sat on a table nearby, but it had burned low and would soon go out.

The witch let go of my hand and pushed me farther into the room. I stumbled but caught myself before I could fall.

"Rest, pretty thing, for your belly is full. Nothing will harm you tonight, unless you wake before daylight."

She slammed the door, and the candle went out.

Alone, I placed my hands on the bed and recoiled instantly. The coverlet was damp, and so were the pillows. I would not rest there and instead lay down on the floor by the bed. It was like sleeping in the kitchen at home, and I suppose it was that familiarity—and my exhaustion from the evening spent with Lore—that helped me sleep despite my awful surroundings.

———

I was torn from slumber by a sudden, sharp kick to my side. I woke trying to catch my breath and full of terror as a terrible shriek filled the room and the witch crashed to the floor beside me. With horror, I realized I had forgotten the fox's final task. I had failed to stretch seven lengths of golden thread from the door to the bed.

Still gasping for breath, I rolled onto my hands and knees and tried to rise to my feet, but the witch wrapped her hands around my ankle, and it was then I realized that she had claws, for they were sharp and cut into my skin. I screamed as the pain sliced through me and she pulled me to the ground.

I fell flat, and my lungs felt paralyzed in my chest. I couldn't even scream as I lost the ability to take in air.

I tried to rise again, but the witch jerked me toward her.

"Pretty creature, full of vicious fae," the witch seethed. "I will cut them out of you. I will drain you dry, but first I will take your eyes."

I rolled onto my back. Though the witch still had her claws in my leg, my other was free, and I used it to kick her. I wasn't sure where my foot landed, maybe her hands or her arms, but she screamed and screeched and finally let me go. I scrambled to my feet, but my leg gave out as I tried to run, shredded by the witch's claws. I rose again and stumbled into the hallway, hitting the wall.

"Lore! Lore, please, help me!"

My scream broke into a sob.

"He cannot hear you, pretty thing," the witch sang in a shrill voice. "He is dead, dead asleep!"

But I knew otherwise. He had not taken her food or drink.

"Lore!"

My hand had just brushed the door when the witch's claws cut into my arms. I screamed as she threw me to the ground but was quickly silenced as my head struck the edge of the wall. My vision swam with explosions of black, and my stomach turned violently. I rolled onto my side and vomited.

"That is what you get for not listening, pretty thing. You are a fighter, and you are a liar," said the witch.

Her claws sunk into my wounded leg, and all I

managed was a short wail. I did not fight her as she dragged me closer and closer to the hearth where a fire still raged.

When she dropped my leg, she turned her back to me, and it was then I caught sight of something glimmering on the floor.

It was the golden thread.

It must have slipped from my pocket.

I don't know what came over me, but something dark took hold, and all I felt was rage—rage toward everyone who had ever hurt me. It was like all the anger my mother had locked away inside me had suddenly been unleashed, and I felt...violent.

I reached for the thread and rose to my feet, stumbling toward the witch, whose back was still turned to me. With each step, I wound the thread around my hands and pulled it taut. As I came up behind her, I looped it around her neck and pulled it tight. I had meant to strangle her and was prepared for the struggle that would ensue, but the thread cut right through her, and her head slid completely off, falling into the empty sink. A second later, her body fell heavily to the floor.

My breathing was ragged and my ribs hurt, but I stood there numbly with the bloody thread dangling from my hands until I caught movement in the distance. Fox popped out from between the darkness of the trees, the glass ax clasped between his teeth, and Lore opened the stable door just as the sun peeked over the horizon.

Together they made their way across the freshly trimmed field toward the cottage.

I left the sink and went outside, making my way down the steps and to the edge of the garden. Lore raced to my side. He touched my face and then backed away to look at me from head to toe. I think he expected me to burst into tears, but right now, I was beyond that.

"Where is that fucking witch?" he hissed, reaching for his blade.

"She's dead," I said. "I killed her."

Lore's anger melted into shock. The only one who did not seem surprised was the fox, who turned his head to the side as he maneuvered the glass ax to the ground and propped it up against the fence.

"You did not listen, wild one," he said.

"No…I didn't," I said, and then I looked at Lore. "I'm sorry. I know how much you wanted to find the wishing tree."

Lore's brows slammed down over his eyes, and his jaw ticked. He didn't like what I'd said, but I assumed it was because he had not yet realized the witch could not tell us where the wishing tree would appear.

"Do not be so quick to presume," said the fox. "The witch can still show us the way to the tree, but first we must harvest her eyes and her claws."

I looked at Lore and handed him the thread.

CHAPTER ELEVEN
The Final Night

LORE

"Sit, wild one, and let me lick your wounds," said the fox as I made my way up the dilapidated steps.

I ground my teeth, needlessly jealous. I should be grateful that the fox could heal Samara, but all I felt was anger. As much as I wanted to be the one to nurse her back to health, I was the reason she needed it. I had promised to keep her safe, and I had failed miserably.

I was a terrible lover but a worse protector.

That reality struck even harder as I entered the witch's cottage and was overwhelmed by a foul stench. I could not place it exactly, but it was sickly sweet and burned my nose. Bile surged into the back of my throat. It was so instantaneous, I choked as I swallowed it down.

If Samara had managed to spend hours in this cottage, I could stay for a few seconds.

I stepped into the kitchen. There was a trail of blood

on the floor between a rotten wooden table and a large blazing hearth over which a cauldron boiled fiercely. Seeing it filled me with dread. What had the witch had planned for my beloved?

I found her body just beyond the table and her head in the sink. Her face was gray and waxy, but her eyes were open, and she stared back at me just as she had in the field.

I shoved my thumb into the corner of her eye, and when her eye popped from its socket, I tore it loose. I did the same with the second.

After it was done, I stared down at her face before catching sight of a row of knives laid out neatly on the counter, and an anger unlike anything I'd ever felt burned through me. I reached for one and before I could think twice, I shoved it deep into the witch's face. I jerked it loose and did it again.

And again.

And again.

I slammed the blade into her until I couldn't breathe. When I was finished and her face was nothing more than a bloody pulp, I screamed until my voice gave out, dissipating into silence.

"Feeling better?" asked the fox.

I wondered at what point he had decided to join me.

"No," I growled. I scooped up the eyes I'd removed from the witch and threw them at the fox. "Here are your fucking eyes."

They landed at his feet. He watched them roll away until they disappeared under the table and then looked at me.

"They are your eyes, Prince of Nightshade," said the fox.

I knew it, but I did not want it to be true. At this moment, I could not understand my own actions. I did not know why I had sent Samara back to this cottage, especially after the night we had shared. I had made love to her. I had made love to her, and no one else had before, and I had let her leave my side to sleep in a house of horror.

I should have kept her by me. I should have spent the rest of the night inside her.

Instead, I had traded all that for a pair of eyes I could barely look at.

"She apologized to me," I said, grinding my teeth so hard my jaw ached. "She, bloody and broken, apologized to *me*."

"What do you expect from a woman who is used to abuse?"

My eyes burned.

Only one thing was clear to me now. Cursed or not—I did not know anymore—nothing changed the fact that I was unworthy of Samara's true love.

"We had better be on our way," said the fox. "Find her eyes, and cut her nails. Tonight, we will find where the wishing tree will grow."

The fox turned and left the cottage, and I followed soon after, but not before dropping the witch's head into her boiling cauldron and setting her cottage alight.

———

We traveled until the sun went down. Fox led the way, and Samara followed. As usual, I lingered behind, carrying the satchel, which felt strangely heavy, weighed down by the witch's eyes and her long iron claws.

Though I desired to walk beside my beloved, it felt like a reward I didn't deserve, so I kept my distance, and she kept hers. I wondered how she felt about me now, in the aftermath of my failure. Did she regret giving herself to me? Did she love me less? Did she love me at all?

The questions gnawed at me the longer we went without speaking, but I could not bring myself to ask. I was afraid and ashamed.

Coward, I thought.

The sun was setting when we stopped at the base of a hill where there were many trees, and the foliage was dense.

"This will do," the fox announced. "Make a fire beneath those shrubs, and burn the witch's eyes. The ashes will tell us where to go."

I hesitated, watching Samara continue on, up the grassy hill and out of sight. I dropped the satchel to the ground and started to follow her, but the fox stopped me.

"Where are you going, Prince of Nightshade?"

"I no longer care about the eyes or the wishing tree," I said. "What value do they hold when all they will do is take my beloved from me?"

"Are you saying you no longer believe you are cursed, prince?" he asked. "Or are you saying you are content to be cursed?"

I hesitated. I did not know exactly what I was saying, I only knew that when I thought of a life without Samara, it was not a life I wanted to live.

"Think carefully before you choose to end this journey," said the fox. "For your beloved has made sacrifices in your name. Would you have her do so in vain?"

"Of course not," I said, frustrated by the fox's question.

"Then burn the eyes, Prince of Poison."

I ground my teeth and set to work, building a small fire beneath the thickest green shrubs, hoping to conceal most of the smoke. I had no idea where Samara's brothers might be in relation to us, and despite having set the witch's cottage on fire, I did not want to give away our current location. While I had failed to protect her from the old woman's evil, I would not fail to protect her from her brothers.

Once the fire blazed, I tossed the eyes into the flames. They were still sticky and wet, and they sizzled until they popped. The fire hissed in retaliation, and the smell made my stomach turn, but I watched them until the fire died. When they were cool, the fox instructed me to pour water over them.

As I did, he watched.

I wondered what he saw in the remains, because all I could make out were ashes swirling. After a few seconds, he gave a soft hum and spoke.

"The wishing tree will appear in a valley surrounded by the Glass Mountains."

I could not deny the dread I felt at the mention of the Glass Mountains, and it reinforced my belief in my curse. The mountains were vengeful, and they had cursed many of my brothers. Why would I be any different?

"Which valley?" I asked. The Glass Mountains went on for miles and miles.

"The moon will let us know," said the fox. "The question you must answer, dear prince, is how will you spend this final night."

Final night.

Those words tore through me.

I did not want a final night with Samara. I wanted many nights—many like the one we'd had last night, but would that be possible on the other side of this broken curse? Right now, I could not imagine feeling anything less for Samara than I felt now. I could not imagine a world without her. She was everything to me—the sun rose and set with her, and the moon waxed and waned with her.

She was the love of my life and even if she broke the curse, that would still be true.

The fox curled up on the ground to sleep while I made my way up the hill where I found Samara sitting, her knees pulled tight to her chest. She was surrounded by tulips, the petals of which seemed to glow pale blue beneath the starlight. As I stared at her from a distance, I remembered the day I'd first laid eyes on her and how she had ensnared me. It was not even her beauty, which was so plainly evident, that hurt my heart. It was what radiated from within her—a kindness I had never seen, a patience I had never endured. Still, she showed these things to me, though I did not deserve them, but tonight I was going to ask for both again as I approached and sat down beside her.

She did not look at me, keeping her head tilted toward the sky.

"Have you learned where we will go next?" she asked, her voice light.

I did not know what to make of it, but I answered her question.

"Yes."

She said nothing, and in the quiet that followed, I gathered the courage to speak.

"I do not want to find the wishing tree," I said.

She looked at me. "Why?"

"Because I do not want to live without you," I said.

She smiled at me, but there was no humor in her eyes or in what she said. "You are a beautiful man," she said. "But you are very stupid."

I frowned. "I am telling you that I do not want to live in a world where I do not love you."

"I know what you are saying," she said. "But you do not seem to understand the point. You still believe your love for me is a curse, which is why we must continue to the wishing tree."

"Why does it matter? I love you now," I said, frustrated.

"It matters because you are afraid of what comes after the wish is made," she said, and then she moved suddenly, shifting into my lap. She wound her arms around my neck, her breasts pressed against my chest, and I tilted my head back to hold her gaze. "But I am not afraid. I am not afraid at all."

Then her mouth was on mine, and something inside me broke open. It was like all the hope I'd locked away within me was suddenly free, pouring into every part of my body, and for the first time since I'd started this journey, I thought that perhaps I had a chance at true love, but with that feeling rose doubt.

"I failed you," I said, breaking our kiss. "I should never have sent you away last night."

"Nothing would have happened if I had listened to the fox," she said.

"It is not about whether you listened," I said. "I chose the quest over you."

Samara's brows lowered. "Do you really believe that?" she asked.

I was surprised she didn't.

"You would never have sent me into that cottage if you thought I was unsafe," she said. "I know that to be true."

It wasn't untrue, certainly.

"It was not fair to you," I said. "I should have kept you at my side, I should have made love to you all night."

"Should have, would have," she said. "There is nothing for you to do except make up for it tonight."

I shook my head, wondering how I had been given such a gift.

"You are incredible," I said.

"I love you," she said, as if she were answering why.

Our lips collided, and I let my hands side up her thighs and beneath her dress. I gripped her ass and pulled her over my arousal.

She pushed me down into the flowers with a firm hand on my chest but did not follow. I stared up at her with a raised brow.

"Samara," I said.

"Yes?" she asked, grinding against my cock.

I let out a hissing breath. "I want to be inside you." She laughed.

"Do you find pleasure in my torture?" I asked.

She made another breathless sound and then bent to kiss my chest.

"No, but I fear I am being selfish tonight," she said. "For I very much desire to taste you as you tasted me."

I groaned and felt my cock tighten a little more, her body grazing me as she kissed down my stomach. It took everything to keep still as she unlaced the ties of my trousers. I distracted myself by removing my prosthetic. It was easier to move without it, but also, my stump was far softer.

My arousal sprang free and the cool air was a welcome relief, but not for long, because soon Samara's hand was wrapped around me, and her thumb was teasing the crown of my cock.

"I should have known from the start you were a siren," I said.

"I am no siren," she said, not looking at me but at my arousal. "I do not even know how to do this."

Even if she did nothing else, I would be content, but then she bent and licked the come from the tip of my cock.

I groaned. "What has made you so bold, wild one?"

She smiled a little. "Curiosity," she said, and then she swirled her tongue around me. "Do you like that?"

A strangled laugh left me. I could barely think. "Yes, wild one," I said. "I love it."

She did it again but continued to explore me with her tongue, running it along every part of me—beneath my crown and along the veins, down to my throbbing balls. I was in disbelief as I watched her. There was a joy to the way she teased and tested, and it was far more arousing than anything I'd ever experienced in my life.

Finally, I could take it no longer, and I pulled her away.

"Enough, wild one. I want to be inside you before I come."

She crawled up my body and straddled me, her mouth closing over mine before sitting back. Then she pulled her dress over her head and tossed it aside. Her skin was pale in the moonlight but marked with bruises. They scored her skin, a map of where I'd explored her last night. It seemed fox's healing had not reached them.

She stared down at me, hesitant. It was the first time since starting this that she didn't seem too confident.

"What is it, beloved?" I asked.

"I...how do you want me?"

"What a wild question," I said. "Any way I can have you, beloved, but I think that tonight, you should stay just where you are."

She looked down, as if she were trying to figure out how we were going to make this work.

"Lean forward a little," I said. "And guide me inside like last night."

She did as I instructed, obedient as ever and eager to please. A wave of heat rushed straight to my head as the crown of my cock sank into her wet heat.

"That's it," I whispered, wanting more of her. My hand smoothed over her ass, gripping her flesh.

She pushed against me, taking me little by little. When she finally sat back, I slid fully inside her, and perspiration had broken out all over my body. I wanted to take a deep breath, but I couldn't until she stopped adjusting to me. Finally, with her hands planted on my stomach and her breasts crushed between her arms, she looked at me.

"Are you okay?"

My laugh was short and hoarse. "I am fine, beloved. Are you?"

She nodded, and I rested my hand and limb on her thighs. At first, she only rocked her hips back and forth, but as she became more comfortable, she started to move up and down my cock, and her breasts bounced. I reached for them, and she bent forward so I could take them into my mouth. I sucked her nipples hard, and she moaned, grinding against me.

I fell back into the flowers and brought her with me, tightening my arms around her and rolling, pinning her beneath me. She anchored her legs around my waist as I thrust into her. I had no thoughts. My only guides were her body and breath as I chased the pressure building at the base of my cock, and when she tightened around me, I came.

I collapsed on top of her, my body shaking. She kept herself wrapped around me, her fingers threading through my now-damp hair as I listened to the beat of her heart. My eyes grew heavy, and as I drifted off to sleep, I thought I heard Samara singing.

CHAPTER TWELVE
Apples Dipped in Gold

SAMARA

A terrible sound startled me awake. I lay there for a few seconds on my side, my back to Lore's chest, listening as my heart raced in my chest. Then I heard it again. It was a cry, short and pained.

"Did you hear that?" I whispered.

"Ignore it," Lore replied, his voice still groggy from sleep. His grip tightened around my waist. He didn't even react when the scream sounded again.

"Lore!" I snapped, elbowing him in the stomach. "There is a woman in trouble!"

He groaned and released me. I sat up.

"It isn't a woman," he said, "It's the fucking fox."

"What?"

"It's about time you two woke up. I have been screaming for half an hour."

I looked ahead to see the fox sitting amid the tulips, staring at us.

"Fuck you," said Lore.

"I am only fulfilling your demand, prince," said the fox. "Tonight is the first night of the full moon and your only chance to end your curse."

"A choice I am regretting by the second," said Lore.

"Take heed, Prince," he said. "Without me, you may have never even met your beloved."

"By all means, Fox, take all the credit."

"I will wait for you at the bottom of the hill," said the fox.

I turned and looked at Lore. He lay on his back, staring at the sky. It was barely morning, but thick clouds hung heavy overhead, and the air smelled like rain.

I moved over him, though I questioned if it was the best decision. His arousal was hard beneath me.

"Are you okay?" I asked.

His violet eyes met mine, his stare striking deep.

"I don't want you to do this," he said.

I was glad he did not lie.

I leaned over him and kissed him softly, whispering against his lips.

"I know."

———

We dressed and headed down the hill where Fox was waiting as promised.

Without a word, he led us up another hill. This one was taller, and once we reached the top, he paused and nodded toward the horizon. Despite the dreary day, I could just make out a faint glimmer in the distance.

"Can you see them?" asked the fox. "Those are the Glass Mountains."

"They seem so far away," I said just as the wind picked up. A chill shivered down my spine.

"Those are the tallest peaks," said Lore. "The range is much closer."

"You have been before?" I asked.

"Regrettably," he said. "The Elder Kingdom lies beyond them. It is where I grew up."

I was surprised. "I didn't realize… But then…how are you Prince of Nightshade?"

"I was designated Prince of Nightshade by my father," he said.

"And where is your father?" I asked.

"He is dead."

The news gave way to a new worry. "I thought fae could not die."

"They can if they choose," said Lore. He paused and then met my gaze. "If anything happened to you, I would choose to die."

I didn't know what to make of his words.

"Don't say that," I whispered.

He was quiet, and there was a sincerity in his eyes that twisted in my gut. Then he slipped his fingers between mine and held my hand as we continued down the other side of the hill and into the forest ahead, though we could not maintain our connection long. The forest was too thick, the underbrush a tangle of brambles and green briar, which not only covered the ground but grew upward into the trees. The stems were impossible to escape; even when I thought I had avoided the sharp thorns, they still managed to scrape across my skin. In some places, the vines were so thick, we had to find a way around.

As we continued through the wood, a horrible smell reached us. It was distinct, putrid and vile, worse even than the witch's cottage.

"What is that horrible stench?" I asked.

"It is the dead," said Lore.

"The dead?" I asked, feeling the blood drain from my face.

"There are dead at the base of the mountains," said Lore. "Many have tried to scale them, and many have failed."

I considered asking why so many had tried to climb the mountains, but I guessed it was likely for the same thing we were after—wishes.

"You do not have to do this, Samara," Lore said.

"I know," I said. "I am choosing to do this, Lore. I will be fine. Fox has not led us astray yet."

At least, that is what I kept telling myself.

That, and I was closer than ever to the truest love I had ever known.

It was nightfall when we broke through the final row of trees. My calves stung, and my skin was shredded and bloody. I was so exhausted, I wanted to collapse, but the moon was out, and she had cast a silver beam of light upon the earth just as the fox had said, only it was guiding us over the first mountaintop, which, as I tilted my head all the way back, seemed to nearly touch the sky.

The height was daunting, but so were the bodies at the base of the mountains, just as Lore had said.

"Fasten the witch's claws to your hands and feet," said the fox. "And you will be able to scale the mountains."

Lore pulled the satchel over his head and withdrew

the claws. They were still bloody. I did not have the heart to ask if it was mine.

We each took four and did as the fox instructed. With two remaining, Lore slid one in my hair as he leaned in to kiss me.

"Just in case," he murmured against my lips.

Our gazes locked as he pulled away, thumb brushing over my cheek. His eyes were dark, almost swallowed whole by his pupils, and there was a tightness to his mouth that made me think there was more he wanted to say, but I would never know what was poised on the end of this tongue, because his body jerked suddenly, and he roared in pain.

"Lore!" I screamed, fear pounding through my entire body as he reached behind his shoulder and snapped off the shaft of an arrow.

My heart raced at the sight of the familiar fetching. It was Michal's.

I whirled, finding my brothers standing before us.

It had only been seven days since I last saw them, but in that time, they had grown far more severe. Anger settled deep in the lines on their faces, and they looked worn and haggard, their cheeks and lips chapped.

They'd had no one to care for them, and they looked every bit as wretched as they were.

The only one I cared about was who stood behind them—Rooster, my sweet and beautiful stallion.

"I cannot believe it is true," said Hans.

"The little whore really did run away with her lover," said Michal.

I glared at them and stepped in front of Lore, though he quickly pulled me back.

My brothers laughed.

"It seems he has made her brave," said Hans with a laugh.

"I have seen that look before," said Michal, lifting his chin. "It is his cock has made her brave."

A low growl escaped from Lore's mouth, but the sound only made Hans and Michal laugh. Jackal was quiet, but his eyes were full of hatred, and his mouth curled in disgust. It was his silence that scared me the most, his silence that made me wary of what he had planned.

"You think you can battle us, demon?" asked Michal.

Hans chuckled, eyes sparking with humor. "We have hunted and survived this forest for many years."

"So has he," I said through gritted teeth.

Hans and Michal exchanged a look.

"We have a lot to beat out of her," said Michal.

"Where do we start?" asked Hans. "With her lover?"

"No," said Jackal. His tone was too calm for what he intended. He drew his knife—Lore's knife—and grabbed Rooster's reins.

"No!" I screamed, lurching forward, only to be held back by Lore.

The stallion jerked sideways, but Jackal yanked him closer, moving to thrust his blade into Rooster's neck, but all of a sudden, Fox was there. He launched himself at Jackal and bit down on his forearm.

Jackal screamed, and Hans and Michal turned in surprise just as Rooster kicked his front feet. The two stumbled back to avoid his strike.

"Samara," Lore snapped, his hand on my forearm. "Climb!"

I hesitated, desperate. I did not want to leave him and Fox to face my brothers.

"Please," I begged, finishing my plea in my head. *Do not leave me.*

It wasn't that I did not trust Lore's skill, but my brothers were motivated by a will to see me suffer and it made them strong.

Lore gripped the back of my head and pressed his lips to my forehead. "I know," he said. "Now go!"

With a final look, I turned and raced to the foot of the mountain, piled high with a mix of bleached bones and swollen and rancid bodies. I retched as I navigated the climb, battling maggots and flies and slipping on loose flesh. My eyes watered from the stench, and my throat burned. I did not know how I made it to the top, but the horror of it all made me desperate to put distance between myself and the corpses.

I pressed my hands against the smooth surface of the glass and then slammed my right foot into the mountainside. The witch's claw sank deep with a strange clink, then I lifted my left hand and stabbed the other claw into its surface. With two secured, I began my climb. It was tedious and terrifying. I hated the strange grind of metal sinking into glass. I gritted my teeth with each movement, sure that by the time I reached the peak, I'd have ground them to dust.

It wasn't long before my hands began to bleed. At first, it was only a few drops, but soon it spilled down the side of the mountain in rivulets. My breathing became ragged, and my body shook. I was tiring quickly, and I had not even made it halfway.

As my will weakened, so did my hope.

I looked down, eyes searching the ground below for Lore, who was locked in battle with Michal. Rooster had Jackal cornered near the base of the mountain, but my sweet stallion kept his distance, too afraid of his weapon, Lore's gleaming knife, to get close.

I turned my attention back to climbing, but I had only made a few more feet when I heard a terrible yelp from below. I looked down despite a wave of dizziness barreling through me to see the fox lying on his side. Hans stood over him, and I screamed.

"No!"

My brother whirled, grinning wildly.

"What's the matter, little whore? Did I kill your pet?" he yelled back, his terrible laugh echoing around me.

A terrible pain ripped through my chest, but as I watched, I noticed something strange. The fox's fur was fluttering, as if caressed by the wind, and then suddenly, he transformed into a human man. He was naked and he had a swath of reddish hair. His eyes blinked open. He lay there for a moment and then reached for a nearby rock. Rising to his feet, he slammed it against Hans's head.

My brother went rigid and fell down dead.

The fox, who was now a man, looked up at me.

"Hurry, Samara!"

It was then I looked to see that Jackal had begun to climb the mountain behind me. Panic shot through my limbs, and all of a sudden, I felt numb. I looked up, still unable to see the top of the Glass Mountains, but the fear of Jackal catching up to me spurred me on. It was fuel that did not last the higher I climbed.

My mouth grew dry, and my lips chapped. I found it hard to swallow, and each attempt to move higher made my entire body shake. Then I felt the brush of fingers against my foot. I looked down to see that Jackal had caught up with me.

It was the shock I needed.

"Don't fucking touch me!" I screamed, scrambling higher.

"I gave you a place to sleep and food to eat," Jackal said, his voice trembled with anger, "I gave you more than you deserved and it was still not enough."

"I gave you everything!" I yelled. My breaths came in wild, wheezing gasps as I tried to climb, though everything in me wanted to stop. "I gave you soft beds and warm rooms, I gave you hot meals and cold beer. I washed your clothes and cut your hair. I kept house like mother did—"

"Do not speak of her!" Jackal yelled so loud, the mountains shook beneath me. "You may look like her and sound like her and move like her, but you are not her. You could never be!"

"Fuck you," I said, and as I looked down at him, I spit in his face.

Jackal roared. "You forget your place, fairy fucker!"

"You're wrong," I said as he neared, pausing my ascent. He glared at me, his teeth bared. "I found my fucking place."

His eyes, full of rage, widened with fear as I let myself drop, smashing my feet into his face. His screams echoed as he fell until his body slammed against the mountain slope. He landed with a final crack atop the pile of corpses at the bottom.

In the silence that followed, all I could hear was my ragged breathing, and then I opened my mouth and began to wail. I had never uttered such a sound, but it came from deep inside me, tearing at my lungs and my throat, and when I could no longer make it, I sobbed.

I don't know how long I clung to the side of the

mountain, but I felt unable to move. My hands were sticky but also dried with blood, and the parts of my skin that touched the mountain were raw. I felt as though I was melting, fusing with the glass beneath me.

My thoughts turned to Lore and the fox and Rooster. I could no longer see the ground, as thick clouds had gathered below me. I wondered if they were alive. I prayed that they were, though I had never really believed in a God.

My eyes grew heavy with exhaustion.

"Samara!"

Lore's voice echoed around me. It sounded so far away, I thought I had only imagined it. Perhaps I had started to slip into a dream or maybe even accepted death's embrace, but then I heard it again.

"Samara, beloved, I am coming!"

Hope swelled in my chest.

He was alive! He was alive, and he was coming for me!

"Lore! Lore, I am here!" I called. "I am waiting!"

I could have cried with happiness, but I had no tears left. The feeling was short lived, however, as a massive shadow passed over me. I looked up to see a large, black raven circling overhead. I had forgotten Cardic's caution, about the raven who guarded the wishing tree and his iron talons.

He gave a sharp cry and then sank his awful claws into my shoulders.

"Lore!"

My scream curdled even my blood as the raven carried me higher and higher, his claws digging deeper as he rose over the mountain's peak. My terror gave way to wonder as I came to see the silver beam of moonlight flooding the valley below.

Where the light touched, everything was green, not glass, and at its center, I saw it.

The wishing tree.

It was more beautiful than I had imagined.

The trunk was massive and the roots were deep. The branches too were long and thick and dense with evergreen foliage and large golden apples. They were so bright against the dark leaves, they almost blinded me.

The raven carried me near, but panic rose inside me as I realized I couldn't let this creature take me any farther, but I had no idea how I was going to get down with his claws locked so keep inside me.

"Please," I tried to speak, but my throat was so dry, I could not raise my voice.

Then I remembered the claw. The one Lore had threaded into my hair as he kissed me goodbye.

I reached to pull it free, screaming through the pain as I hacked at the raven's feet. The bird gave a harsh cry and released me just as he flew over the wishing tree.

I fell, hitting the branches as I landed hard on my back.

I knew I was broken as I lay there on the ground, yet I felt no pain, only wonder as I stared up at the emerald canopy, heavy with golden fruit.

Something dropped near me, and I turned my head to the side. An apple had fallen within reach. I stretched, grazing its smooth skin with my fingertips, rolling it closer until I could take it in hand. I held it against my heart, and closed my eyes, wishing that Lore was no longer cursed.

Then I took a bite.

The skin was crisp and broke easily, flooding my mouth with sweetness.

It was the last thing I remembered and nothing more.

CHAPTER THIRTEEN
True Love's Kiss

LORE

"Samara!"

I don't know how many times I screamed her name and waited for a reply, but nothing came.

Still, I continued, clinging to the hope that she was alive on the other side of the mountain. I did not even care if she'd found the wishing tree. I did not care if she had eaten an apple or made a fucking wish.

All I wanted was for her to be alive.

"Why isn't she answering?"

"Do not think on it, Prince, just keep going," said Fox—or rather, Friedrich, who was not a fox at all, but a man cursed to live as a fox. After I'd managed to cut Michal's throat, I'd come face to face with him and punched him in the face.

"What was that for?" he'd demanded, holding a hand to his cheek.

"I warned you when you slept on Samara's bed that you had better be a fox," I said.

Now he climbed the mountain behind me, dressed in Samara's brothers' clothes.

"I heard her scream," I said. "I know the raven has taken her. Fuck!"

I wanted to stop. I wanted to beat my fist against this fucking mountain until I shattered it into a thousand pieces but that was not possible, so I kept climbing.

When we reached the very height of the Glass Mountains, the sun shone brilliantly on the horizon, and in the distance, I could see the dazzling turrets of my father's castle. It had been a long time since I'd looked upon his golden castle, though it held little interest as I hugged the narrow peak of the mountain, finally making it to the other side.

Relief washed over me as I observed the valley below, but I was soon overcome with panic as I saw Samara lying beneath the branches of a skeletal tree.

"Samara!" I screamed, but she did not move. "Samara! Fuck!"

I pulled my claws from the glass and sailed down the side of the mountain.

As I neared the bottom, I shoved them into the mountain to slow my descent. The sound tore at my insides, but again, I did not care. Once my feet touched the ground, I nearly fell as I raced to my beloved, falling to my knees beside her.

She was pale, her face void of color and her lips blue.

"Samara!" I breathed, shaking her before pressing my ear to her chest, but there was no heartbeat, no signs of life.

"No," I said as a keen wail tore from my throat. I gathered her into my arms, tucking her head beneath my chin, rocking her back and forth. "No, please! This cannot be. Please come back. Please don't leave me."

"Oh, Prince," said Friedrich as he approached.

I pulled away and stared at Samara's beautiful face through my tears.

"I love her, Friedrich," I said. "I love her, and I never told her."

"Tell her now, Prince," he said. "Tell her and kiss her."

I took a shaky breath and rested my forehead rest against hers. "I was wrong to never say it, wrong to never believe it. I love you, Samara. I love you more than anything in this terrible world."

I kissed her, though she was cold, and then I held her to me and willed her to be warm.

It was only a moment after that I felt her fingers in my hair and heard her speak my name. I pulled away to find her eyes open, her cheeks and lips as rosy as they were before.

"Lore," she whispered and placed her palm flat against my cheek. She looked at me in wonder, as if I were the miracle.

"Samara," I said, holding her face in my hands, marveling at the life in her beautiful blue eyes. "You are not a curse at all but a gift. You are my dream come true and my greatest wish. I love you. I have loved you since the moment I saw you seven years ago."

"I know," she said and smiled so sweetly, I could not help kissing her.

She pulled away and gasped, looking over my shoulder where I knew Friedrich stood.

"Who are you?" she asked.

"I am Fox," he said, bowing. "Or Friedrich if you'd like."

She opened her mouth to speak, but I stopped her. "Pretend he doesn't exist." I said and kissed her again, longer this time. I was slow to stop, letting my lips linger against hers.

"Marry me, Samara of Gnat," I said when I pulled away.

She smiled and answered, "No."

"What? Why not? We love each other, do we not?"

"I will marry you eventually," she said. "But only after you have lived with me in my quiet cottage by the moor for at least a year."

"Beloved," I said, nuzzling her nose with mine. "Your heart is my home. I will go wherever you lead."

And they lived happily ever after.

Author's Note

Hello and welcome to my TedTalk—as you are all probably used to by now, I have a lot to tell you about the fairy tales that influenced this story, and like *Mountains Made of Glass*, there are many.

First, I want to say this story was far more complicated than *MMOG* for a variety of reasons. I tend to write first books in a series as more straightforward romances and I thought every book in this series, since they all feature a different couple, would be just as simple...but I was wrong. This one took a toll on me mentally, and I think a huge part of that was the abuse Samara suffered, particularly at the beginning of the story. Abuse—mental, physical, sexual, and neglect—is prevalent across fairy tales. It is said that the Brothers Grimm were the first to include these themes in literature to reflect the historical and social context of the time. I do want to note again that the Brothers Grimm collected fairy tales, they did not write them, so this suggests only that they chose to include fairy tales with child abuse, not exclude them.

Abuse was also featured heavily in *The Hand with the Knife* by the Brothers Grimm which is the fairy tale that inspired most of *Apples Dipped in Gold*. In the story, a maiden is horribly abused by her brothers and mother and is forced to cut peat from the bog with a dull knife. An Elf falls in love with the girl and offers her a knife that can cut anything in two but when the girl starts to finish her chore faster than before, her brothers and mother grow suspicious. The brothers follow her and discover the hand with the knife. They force her to give them the knife and cut off the Elf's hand and he is never seen again.

I thought this was an intriguing beginning to a story and so, in my head, *Apples Dipped in Gold* is what happens in the aftermath. Though the events I just described happen before the start of his fairytale, they are referenced heavily throughout the novel.

Other Grimm Fairy Tales

There are a few other Grimm fairy tales I referenced throughout the book. Notably, *The Nixie of The Mill-Pond* where a miller meets a woman in his mill pond. She had a beautiful voice and promised to make him rich if he brought her "the young thing which has just been born in your house." He agrees because he thinks that it must be a puppy or kitten, not knowing that his wife just gave birth to a son. The miller warns his son to stay away from the pond and he does, of course, until one fateful day hunting. When he vanishes, he has left behind his beloved who is given a golden comb and told to comb her long, black hair beneath the moonlight by the mill pond. She is given other tasks after this—play a flute, spin this spinning wheel. Eventually, her persistence pays off and her beloved rises from the pond. There is more to this story—the two forget each other and must remember but the themes here—the alluring voice, the comb, and later, moonlight—are obvious and appear also in *Apples Dipped in Gold*.

There is another story called *The Water-Nixie* which is about a brother and sister who are captured by a water-nixie who lives in a well. She forces them to work for her but after some time, they are able to escape. As they run from her, the children throw items at the creature to stop her—a brush, a comb, a mirror. Each item stops the nixie from pursuing them, though not as violently as I portrayed in *Apples Dipped in Gold* (though we know these fairy tales could be just as terrible).

One of the reasons I have the comb turned into a thousand spears is because in *The Water-Nixie* the comb is said to "make a great ridge with a thousand times a teeth."

The next fairy tale I want to talk about is *The Golden Bird*. In this story, there is a king and three sons who all try to discover who is stealing golden apples from a tree in the garden. Only the youngest is able to witness a golden bird pluck an apple from the tree. He was also able to shoot the bird, but only one of his golden feathers fell to the ground.

The feather was so valuable, the king desired the entire thing and so the sons set out to find the golden bird. Once again, the youngest is the only one who can accomplish the task, though he would not have done so without a Fox who counsels him along the way. The advice the fox gives is always very straightforward. For example, at one point he tells the brothers "this evening you will come to a village in which stand two inns opposite to one another. One of them is lighted up brightly, and all goes on merrily within, but do not go into it; go rather into the other, even though it looks like a bad one." Of course, two of the brothers enter the "good" inn and the youngest enters the "bad" inn.

Later, the fox will tell the youngest son to walk straight past a regiment of soldiers and into the castle where the bird is held. While there is an empty golden cage, the boy is warned to keep the bird in the "common cage." The young prince does not listen and as soon as he tries to move the bird from cage to cage, he squawks and wakes the soldiers.

The young prince's journey continues after that with the fox advising and while he has not been proven wrong by the fox's guidance, he continues to ignore it for some reason. It's very frustrating. Finally, though, at the end of the story the fox asks the youngest son to kill him and chop off his head and feet. The prince obliges and when he does, the fox becomes a man and of course, he, too, is a prince.

Obviously, you can see the parallels between the fox in *Apples Dipped in Gold* and the fox in *The Golden Bird*. He advises as if he already knows how everything plays out. There is no explanation for why he has this knowledge, and no one ever questions it, though as soon as he is not obeyed, there are great consequences as we saw with Samara and the witch.

Hans Christian Andersen

As I indicted in the author's note of *Mountains Made of Glass*, Hans Christian Andersen is noted for creating his own fairy tales, but they also have similar tones and themes.

The fairy tale I used most in *Apples Dipped in Gold* is called *The Elf-Mound.* I highly recommend reading it after you have read this retelling not only because it is fun, but you will see the parallels.

The story is initially observed from the point of view of the lizards who see that something is taking place at the elf mound. They were kept awake all night by a grand commotion and are discussing it as an 'old-maid elf' emerges from the elf mound. She is hurrying to see the night-raven and invites him to the mound if he will do them a favor and deliver invitations. She goes into a very long-winded explanation about who can come to the ball and banquet and who should be invited and why or why not. I used this same behavior pattern when Lore encounters the old elf maid in *Apples.*

In the exchange, the "old-maid elf" invites "the old man of the sea and his daughters" which I took as a reference to Nereus who is named by Homer as, "Old Man of the Sea." His daughters would be the Nereids, or sea nymphs. She also invites the "grave pig" which is the ghost of a pig buried in a church yard. I called this creature a gloson in the book. It is the same creature, though I felt there were more details under the name gloson than grave pig.

The gloson is said to have a razor-sharp saw sticking out of its back and it will charge at its pray and cut them in half.

Anyway, we later learn that the reason there is such a stirring at the Elf-Mound is because the old elf king is receiving the goblin chief of Norway as he desires to find wives for his two sons who are said to be "rough and rowdy." The old elf king tells his daughters, "they'll improve when they get older. It's up to you to polish them." I referenced this exchange when Lore comments to the elf maid, "pity the women they choose."

The expectation that the women are responsible for their husband's behavior is obviously not new—in fairy tales or the modern world.

Andrew Lang

The Yellow Fairy Book by Andrew Lang includes two stories I used in *Apples Dipped in Gold—The Glass Mountains* and *The Glass Axe*.

In *The Glass Mountains*, a princess has been trapped in a golden castle at the top of the Glass Mountains for seven years. A golden apple tree grows before it, and it was said that whoever picked a golden apple from the tree would gain entrance to the castle. Many had tried and failed, to the point that corpses had piled out at the base of the mountains. One day, a young boy appears and desires to rescue the princess, so he cuts off the claws of lynx and begins to scale the mountain. It is a rough climb. Eventually, he is attacked by an eagle who guards the tree. The youth grabs onto his feet and the eagle carries him high over the mountain top. When he is in view of the tree, he cuts the eagle's feet off with a small knife. Though he is injured during his fall, he is able to eat one of the golden apples and heal himself.

In *Apples*, I did not use the claws of a lynx but instead the claws of a witch which is a reference to the Grimm fairy tale, *The Goose Girl at the Well* in which a father warns his sons, "beware of the old woman. She has claws beneath her gloves. She is a witch."

The other fairy tale is *The Glass Axe* in which a young Prince is kidnapped by a fairy queen. She orders him to cut down all the trees there before sunset using only a glass axe.

The first blow he strikes shatters the axe into thousands of pieces. It turns out, the fairy's daughter has been exiled to the woods as well. She finds the young prince and offers to help him with his task. Of course, she has magic and reassembles the glass axe and completes the task.

I had the witch task the fox with a similar favor—a rick of wood by morning—because I needed Samara and Lore alone so they could have sex, LMAO.

Other Themes

Samara has a bit of a "Cinderella" moment when she is found by the dryads and given a dress so she can go to the ball. In Apples, Old Mother gives Samara a walnut. Inside, there is a beautiful dress. This is a reference to a few Grimm fairy tales, *Allerleirauh, The Two King's Children, The Iron Stove*. In each, a princess is given nuts (usually three) with beautiful dresses inside.

I am sure you can pick out a few themes from *Little Snow White*. Samara is made to work hard for her family, and she has black hair and rosy lips. She is also poisoned at the end of the book by an apple. These themes aren't really themes exclusive to Snow White, but the title is a reference to the poisoned apple in *Little Snow White*. In *Apples Dipped in Gold*, it was technically Samara's wish that poisoned her. She wanted Lore free from his curse and the only way to do so was to die and be awakened by true love's kiss. This is more-so a reference to Disney's version of Snow White, since in *Little Snow White*, she was awakened after the apple was dislodged from her throat.

It goes without saying the overall theme of this novel is the concept of love at first sight. I presented this in two ways within *Apples Dipped in Gold*. One was with

Prince Henry who decides to marry Samara at first sight, commenting that she is too beautiful to die. He also adds that "beauty is genius" which is a reference to *The Picture of Dorian Gray*. The actual quote is, "Beauty is a form of Genius—is higher, indeed, than Genius, as it needs no explanation." The irony here is that *The Picture of Dorian Gray* is a story about the corruption of beauty. The beautiful are easily forgiven and easily loved by society.

Because Samara is beautiful, the prince decides she is worthy of his attention, his love, and the title of princess. She thinks he is an idiot, but she is desperate to leave her situation.

On the contrary, we have Lore who does not think that love at first sight exists which is why he believes he is cursed. He can acknowledge that Samara is beautiful, and he is captivated by that beauty, but grows more frustrated the longer he cannot disentangle himself from his feelings. This spurs the entire journey to the Glass Mountains which, at the end, is where he is convinced his love for Samara is real but only after she sacrifices herself.

And yes, Lore is an idiot, but there is something to be said about people who believe in something so much, it becomes true.

If anything, I think these retellings just point out the far-fetched nature of the source material while also shedding light on what society values. There is nothing more disturbing than seeing your world within the pages of two-hundred-year-old fairy tales and realizing it hasn't changed.

As always, I hope you enjoyed this tale because Cardic and his nun are next.

Much love,

Scarlett

References

Andersen, H., Walker, D. and Tegner, H. (2012) *Hans Christian Andersen: Best-loved fairy tales*. New York: Fall River Press.

Grimm, J., Grimm, W. and Hunt, A.W. (2021) *The Complete Grimm's Fairy tales*. New Delhi: FingerPrint! Classics.

Grimm, Jacob, Wilhelm Grimm, Jack Zipes, and Andrea Dezsö. *The Original Folk and Fairy Tales of the Brothers Grimm: The Complete First Edition*. Princeton: Princeton University Press, 2014.

Grimm, J., Grimm, W. and Mondschein, K. (2011) *Grimm's Complete Fairy Tales*. San Diego: Canterbury Classics.

Lang, Andrew. *The Yellow Fairy Book, by Andrew Lang*. New York, NY: First Racehorse for Young Readers, 2020.

Treasury of Irish Fairy and Folk Tales. Barnes & Noble Inc, 2016.

Acknowledgments

My experience with limb loss is secondary. My sister lost her leg below the knee a couple of years ago and the toll it has taken on her emotional, mental, and physical health has been more intense than anything I have witnessed in my life, and yet, she has handled the transition with such grace despite the world catering to able bodies. As I wrote Lore, the other thing I learned is that language is also ableist and I must give credit to my friend and former co-worker, Dave Brown, who answered so many questions about navigating the world with one hand.

Of course, I wouldn't have gotten anything done if it wasn't for my editor, Christa, who graciously opens her home and she shed to me when I find myself stuck and pushing against a deadline. When you reached out to me via email in July of 2021 about joining Bloom, I never guessed I would not only gain a new friend but an entire family. Thank you for welcoming me and my Adie girl.

Thank you to my agents, Caitlin and Alyssa, and my best friends, Ashley and Molly, for giving me the space to write and encouragement along the way, even when I stop being so responsive. Your support is endless and keeps me moving forward

Last, but not least, none of this would be possible without my husband, Armand, who keeps the house clean, cooks, takes care of Adie, and drives me everywhere I need to go when I am on deadline. There is no one in the world more dedicated than you. You are unwavering, even in the face of my chaos. I love you.

To every reader who has read *Apples Dipped in Gold* and loved it as much as I do—thank you from the bottom of my heart for taking a chance on a ridiculous novel. I'm glad you're on this journey with me.

About the Author

#1 *New York Times* bestselling author Scarlett St. Clair is a citizen of the Muscogee Nation and the author of the Hades X Persephone series, the Adrian X Isolde series, Fairy Tale Retellings, and *When Stars Come Out*.

She has a master's degree in library science and information studies and a bachelor's in English writing. She is obsessed with Greek mythology, murder mysteries, and the afterlife. For information on books, tour dates, and content, please visit scarlettstclair.com.